P9-AQU-664

MICK. Born a blue-eyed son, a life in his close-knit Irish community has already been mapped out for him. But what if it's a life he has no stomach for? Can he tear up the map and throw it away?

SULLY. He's always been Mick's best friend. He's always followed Mick's lead. But now their checkerboard neighborhood is changing, and Mick is moving off the white square of home—into dangerous territory. Should Sully follow? Does he really want to?

EVELYN. She's beautiful and she's a poet. She's also as hard as nails. Mick can't resist her—probably because he's the last thing in the world that she wants.

TOY. He's street-smart and worldly-wise, and nobody messes with him–ever. Mick can't believe how lucky he is to have Toy as a friend. And then he begins to learn some of Toy's closely guarded secrets. . . .

TERRY. Mick's big brother is a violent drunk, and an even more violent bigot. In fact, he's the local hate monger. Lately he's been hating the fact that Mick doesn't want to follow in his footsteps. . . .

Also by Chris Lynch

Shadow Boxer

"A gritty, streetwise novel that is much more than a sports story." (Starred review)
—*School Library Journal*

"The fight sequences, fraternal dynamics, and memorable cast of eccentric characters make for some riveting episodes in this rough, tough-talking book about boxing and brotherhood."
—*The Horn Book*

Iceman

"Much better than the usual sports novel, this is an unsettling, complicated portrayal of growing up. . . . A thought-provoking book guaranteed to compel and touch a teenage audience." (Starred review)
–ALA *Booklist*

"Hockey enthusiasts will enjoy the abundant on-ice action, although this novel is clearly about much more. . . . Iceman will leave readers smiling and feeling good."
—*School Library Journal*

Gypsy Davey

"The dialogue crackles with realism. . . . In terms of literary quality, this work is outstanding." (Starred review) —*School Library Journal*

"Young adults will appreciate [*Gypsy Davey*'s] honesty and fast pace. Lynch steers clear of sensationalism and paints characters who ring true every time."
—*The Bulletin of the Center for Children's Books*

mick

Blue-Eyed Son #1

CHRIS LYNCH

FRANKLIN PIERCE
COLLEGE LIBRARY
RINDGE, N.H. 03461

HarperTrophy

A Division of HarperCollinsPublishers

To Tina,
because she likes this one
better than Iceman

Mick
Copyright © 1996 by Chris Lynch
All rights reserved. No part of this book may be
used or reproduced in any manner whatsoever
without written permission except in the case of
brief quotations embodied in critical articles and
reviews. Printed in the United States of America. For
information address HarperCollins Children's Books,
a division of HarperCollins Publishers, 10 East 53rd
Street, New York, NY 10022.

Library of Congress Cataloging-in-Publication Data
Lynch, Chris
  Mick / Chris Lynch.
      p.   cm. — (Blue-eyed son ; #1)
  Summary: His friendship with two Hispanic stu-
dents offers fifteen-year-old Mick an alternative to
the drunken savagery of his brother and the narrow
thinking of his Irish-American neighborhood in
Boston.
  ISBN 0-06-447121-7(pbk.) — ISBN 0-06-025397-5
(lib. bdg.)
  [1. Prejudices—Fiction.   2. Irish Americans—
Fiction.   3. Boston (Mass.)—Fiction.   4. Alcoholism—
Fiction.]   I. Title.   II. Series: Lynch, Chris.   Blue-eyed
son ; #1.
PZ7.L979739Mi   1996   94-18725
[Fic]—dc20   CIP
                                                    AC

CURR
PZ
7
.L979739
Mi
1996

Typography by Steve Scott
3   5   7   9   10   8   6   4   2

❖

Contents

Part One

Part Two

mick

Part One

🍀

Oughtnotta

"**Y**o man, Sul, you died again this morning," I told Sully. I was telling him that all the time. "Twice, even."

"Ya, I know it. It's this town, this town is killer on us poor Sullies. Gotta get out of this town before we're a lost breed."

I can't help it. I read the obituaries. I read for famous people because when famous people die it's like people I know are dying. I read for old people, like ninety or a hundred years old, just to find out what these people did with all that time, since, myself, I don't know what to do with my time if it gets to be three o'clock on a Saturday and it's raining out. So a hundred years is some *time* to fill. I read for creepy diseases and for violent deaths and for the names of people I know.

Like Sully. There are about three hundred million John Sullivans in this town and one of them croaks nearly every day. Most of them are, like my friend, John J. Sullivan. John J. Sullivan, Jr., John J. Sullivan III, just dead, all over the place. Supposed to be an Irish thing, this reading the death notices, the Irish Sports Pages and all that. I don't know.

We walked up to Baba's house. Baba, as in Baba O'Reilly. As in "Teenage Wasteland." It's a song. Hey, it's better than his real name, which is Ryan. Ryan O'Reilly, now that's pretty stupid isn't it? Anyway, it's accurate, the Teenage Wasteland thing. But Baba's okay. He's got some attitude, but Baba's okay.

"C'mon up, I gutta finish eatin'" Baba yelled down from his kitchen window. He says "eatin'" like it doesn't have a *t* in the middle. EEE-in.

"Well hey," I said as we walked up the creaky staircase, "we get to come up for a quick peanut butter–and-steroid sandwich with Baba." We don't know that Baba takes 'roids, he just looks and acts like someone who does, even though he says he doesn't. He bit somebody on the head once just for asking, so we don't ask.

"Stay away from the peanut butter," Sully

said, stopping me on the stairs and looking very serious.

"What?"

"I said don't eat the peanut butter in this house."

"Why not?"

Sully started to say something, gagged, took a deep breath and a swallow, then spoke. "Listen, I've been there. I've seen things. Just don't eat the peanut butter, all right? Tell me you won't eat the peanut butter."

"I won't, I won't eat it," I laughed, but he had me a little nervous anyway. "Pretty health conscious for a dead guy, Sul."

When we walked into the kitchen, there was hulking Baba eating, of course, a peanut butter sandwich. I couldn't look at it. I looked at the rest of his pre-workout training meal, laid out in front of him on the table. He had twelve different bottles of megavitamins, lined up like toy soldiers. After each bite of sandwich he dumped a few pills from a bottle into his hand, popped them, and chased them with Tang.

"Want some?" Baba said, his food-filled mouth wide open.

I covered my mouth with both hands.

"How can you eat like that right before exercising?" Sully asked. "I'd get sick."

Baba laughed. "I like not bein' all digested when I work out, and havin' all them vitamins in there making my belly all jumpy. It makes me angry. It makes me mean. That's good."

"That's good?" I asked.

"That's good, Bones." Baba is the only one in the world who calls me Bones. Because I'm not skinny. It was just the only response he could think of when I named him Baba. "Mean is good. Mean is strong. Gotta be ready, y'know. Gotta be ready."

"What do we have to be ready for, Baba?"

The conversation was somehow getting him fired up. He always found *something* to get fired up about. He started pouring pills madly into his mouth, swallowing them dry. "Anything," he garbled. "Gotta be ready for anything. Everything." He smiled a knowing smile and winked, as if Sully and I knew too. We didn't.

The three of us went to the gym, like we do a lot. Baba hit the Nautilus machines like an animal, never breaking stride from the time he left his kitchen table till the time he lay flat on his back to bench-press a couple million pounds. He could press almost three hundred pounds on Nautilus, which was about like Sully hanging off one end of a bar and me off the other while Baba jerked us up and down.

"Enough of this diddly shit," Baba growled after five minutes of the machines. He stomped over to the free weights, his real workout, sucking on his water bottle.

"Spot me, Mick," he called. So I left the treadmills, where Sully and I were running side by side.

"What are you gonna do if he can't get it up, Mick? Lift it for him?" Sully said as he ran on without me.

"Nah, he just needs somebody to wave their arms and scream help help, which I can do."

Baba grunted, sipped his water, and pointed at the big round steel weight plates. I loaded them on, forty-fives, twenties, tens, and he pumped them. I looked right down into his face as he forced the weight up another time and another, his face purple, long, green wormy veins bulging out of his neck. Sucking that air in as the weight returned to his mountainous chest, blowing the weight back up again. Sitting up, he did his military presses. Standing, his curls. As I stood behind, no longer with any purpose other than to hang around and admire him, I did just that. We both faced the wall of mirrors as Baba curled the wavy curl bar up to his chin, his lip making the same snarl every time, a twitch only curling gave him. I compared things. His forearms were roughly as thick as my calves, calves I do a lot of work on I might add. His biceps, my thighs. His neck, my waist. He had reddish brown hair all over his body and, at sixteen, already a receding hairline.

"Why do you pump so much, Baba?" I asked; I don't know why. He never gave a decent answer to questions about himself. But he was so intense about it, and didn't play football or hockey or anything that would make it make sense.

He abruptly dropped the weights to the floor with a clang that got us some looks, from guys as big as Baba. Dropping the weights like that is a big no-no around here. A religious kind of thing.

"Feel that," he said, bending his arm and offering me one of his biceps about the size, shape, and firmness of a ten-pound canned ham still in the can.

"It's big," I said.

"It's gutta be *bigger*," he said, and went back to work.

"Oh," I said. "Baba, I'll be back in awhile. I'm gonna do some other stuff."

"Go," he said. "Wimp around."

I met Sully at the butterfly station, halfway through his Nautilus routine. We usually lift together, but since he started without me and since Baba was making me feel kind of like a fly, I bagged it. I pulled on some gloves and smacked around the heavy bag instead. Shortly, Sully joined me, bouncing on his toes and batting the speed bag to the beat of the music filling the room, some boring but steady Guns 'N Roses thump that every musclehead in the place seemed to know all the words to.

As I rapped out a good tom-tom beating on the heavy bag's ribs, Sully tapped an effortless, seamless rhythm on the speed bag, practically floating as his weight drifted perfectly from his right to his left and back, no pausing in one spot, but no herky-jerking either. His sound was like when there are twenty guys in a gym all dribbling basketballs at once.

We stood out, I realized when I stopped for a blow. As I stood hunched with my hands on my knees and Sully's drumming behind me, I couldn't help but notice that nobody in the gym was doing quite what we were doing.

It was a pretty decent gym for a neighborhood place. Had three treadmills and three Stair-Masters, a couple of rowing machines, life cycles all over the place, all great cardiovascular stuff. And all basically unused. Time after time we would come in here and Sully and I would be the only ones to touch any of the best equipment.

Weights. Weights and more weights. This was not a health club, it was a weight club. The hugest people you ever saw came here to get huger. Guys with big round bellies and round red faces who looked just fat until they squatted under the bar and started to pump and the roly-poly arms bulged into something sculptured under that flesh. Four different arms sported the Notre Dame fighting leprechaun tattoo, and countless others had tiny crosses tattooed in the webbing at the base of their thumbs. Smallish ratty guys, the place always crawled with the smallish ratty guys, crew-cut and scarred, with veins up and down their arms like they were running *over* the skin instead of under it. Sinewy, flat-chested guys desperately trying to pack something fearsome onto the small rack of bones they were born with, usually succeeding, as one compact monster after another jerked the bar over his head and held his weight and a half for five or ten seconds with his dense muscles fairly popping through his skin.

High fives and forearm smashes. Guys who wouldn't say hello on the street walked by each other as they strutted all puffed up from a big victory over the bench press toward the dumbbells, and slapped hands, punched fists, nodded righteously at comrades in fat leather weight belts. As if they were now somehow on the same team.

So when Sully and I were running the tread-mills or slapping the bags around making noise, we got a lot of looks. Because the idea here was not to get a well-rounded workout—I saw a guy once lifting with a cigarette hanging out of his mouth—it was to get bigger, bigger, bigger big-ger. I think we were allowed to stay only because we came with Baba, and because we did mix in a little weight work here and there.

But the looks we got were *nothing* compared to what the black guy got. When he walked in, carrying no bag, just to try the place out, every-thing stopped. I mean *everything*. Huge stacks of plates clanged together as somebody dropped a Nautilus bar in mid-lift. The rat spotting for the bear-shaped giant on the bench tapped him on the shoulder and when the bear sat up both of them just stared. Fifteen or twenty guys, their shirts torn, sweat rolling down their necks, fin-gerless gloves on, stood or sat, and stared. Ab-solutely motionless. Including Sully and me.

I saw a million black guys a day, so it wasn't like a novelty or something. And it wasn't like it was a lily-white neighborhood, either, since you could open the door to the gym and throw a rock in one direction and break the window of a black guy's house, throw it in another and hit a Puerto Rican's. It's a mixed neighborhood, but not mixed *up*, you know? Like checkerboard squares. This street is white, the next one is black, the next one after that is Spanish. Sully said it one time, that it's like fudge ripple ice cream—it's all in one box, but it ain't exactly blended.

The thing, though, that I didn't even think about, that I knew but didn't *know* until that black man walked in the door, was that the guy in that house *there* and the guy in that house over *there*, they could live *there*. But they couldn't come in *here*.

It wasn't that it was a *restricted* club or anything. But I just don't know why he'd come. Why he would want to. Because it wasn't his place. I wouldn't want to go to a place that wasn't *my* place, y'know. Maybe he just didn't know.

But he had to have noticed the way every single eye followed him, how nobody but him did a lick of working out, how somebody assumed a stand at every station on the Nautilus, and at most of the free-weight spots, refusing to budge, so that he had to settle for a few sit-ups on the incline bench and some triceps extensions with what weights were left scattered.

Sully went back to hitting his bag first, then I did too. We didn't stop watching the guy, though, and our punches shot out louder than ever in the stillness. Even the headbanger thrash music coming out of the speakers seemed like nothing more than a breeze wafting through.

He was just looking, anyway. Giving it a test run, the way anybody does when they're thinking of joining a club. They should have just left him alone; he would have gone home and told his friends about the place, then they would have told *him* about the place, and everything could be put back normal. But they couldn't let it lie. First to move was Baba. He got up off the weight bench and made a gracious sweeping gesture with his hand to offer it to the guy. The black guy nodded. He didn't smile or anything, but his face lifted somewhat. He took it as an invitation, and lay right down on the bench, with all the weight on it that Baba was lifting even though this guy weighed probably forty pounds less than Baba.

I knew what Baba was thinking. Not that it's cold fusion to figure out what Baba's thinking. But he figured that guy couldn't lift the weight. Baba himself even acted as spotter for the guy, and I knew then that something good wasn't going to happen.

What Baba hadn't planned on, though, was that the guy pressed the weight. Pressed it right up. Not like it wasn't hard or anything, but slow and steady and perfectly balanced. Great form, he wasn't no rookie. Then he brought it down to his chest to do it again.

Baba and the muscle boys stood with their mouths hanging open, which, again, is not that unusual. But it meant something for a change. Almost without moving, a bunch of them pulled in tighter around the guy. And he noticed. They weren't coming to study his form. He got edgy, broke the concentration that made it possible to lift impossible weight. His right arm started going up a little ahead of his left, and there he was cooked. The weight shifted, his right foot came off the floor as he struggled to balance the load, but the whole thing began to sink back down on him.

The music got louder. Somebody was hitting the button. Hitting it, hitting it, juicing it until the walls were ringing with metal, the sound blasting out like the cap off a hot radiator.

"Spot me," the guy called, signaling Baba to help him.

Baba folded his arms, looked straight down on him, and smiled. "Sorry, man, can't hear you with the music."

The man now knew where he was. He didn't ask again. He closed his eyes, took three deep breaths, and when he opened up again, the resolve, the control, the focus was there again. Slowly, and remarkably, the bar began rising off his chest. Three inches up, five. A short pause as he struggled to push it through the halfway point, then he broke it, the weight was up.

But not. Just as the man's elbows were about to lock, Baba reached out his hand and began to push. Down. The man fought back, sweat bubbling all over his face. But it was no use. Baba applied more pressure, and more, as needed and then some, until the man was pinned and gasping, the weight bar lying heavy with the help of several hands now, across his collarbones.

Baba dropped to his knees and breathed right into the guy's face while the others held him down. "Maybe you don't know, but maybe you oughtnotta come here. You understand me, muthuh?"

The man did not respond. The weightlifters leaned harder, until the load included all the weight plus nearly all the poundage of two huge guys. Still, the man did not respond, other than to drop his hands from the bar. His eyes fluttered shut like he was passing out.

Laughing, they removed the weight from him. Slapping his face, happily, Baba and one of the others half revived him and helped him to the door. Once there, they gave him a shove and sent him staggering across the parking lot. He didn't know where he was, just like when he arrived.

Baba strutted back to the deafening roar of whoops and screams. High fives and forearm smashes all around. He stopped short, raised his arms, and sang a screechy chorus of "God Bless America" joined by everybody in the place.

Even Sully. Even, after a glare from Baba, me. I wasn't sure if I loved *this* America so much right about then, but I was sure I loved it better than I loved a punch in the head.

Then they all went back to pumping iron. Harder, faster, meaner than before. Nobody talked to anybody else, but everybody laughed, a lot, at nothing. They were like a scary race of muscle-bound 'droids pumping and laughing, barking and spitting, out of control.

Sully didn't laugh, and neither did I. We never seemed to be able to muster up the same kind of *spirit* those guys had.

Who Are You?

"**C**omin', Mick?"

It wasn't really a question. My brother doesn't usually *ask* me anything. Thought I might answer anyway, though.

"No, I'm not coming."

"Put your damn jacket on. You're comin'."

So I put my damn jacket on. Blue dungaree, like always. If it's seventy out, I wear the blue dungaree. If it snows, the blue dungaree.

"Where's your green? Where's your goddamn green? And your hat?"

"I don't like to wear hats, Terry. They make me feel like I need a shower and I have to keep scratching my head."

17

"Don't gimme no lip. Go back in there and put on the green and white striper. We gotta get goin'."

Where we had to get going to was Terry's bar. Not that he actually *owned* the bar, not quite, anyway. It was just the place where he spent most of his time and all his money. Saw him one time walk in there with his paycheck, sign it, and hand the whole thing right over to the laughing bartender. The bar, a place called Bloody Sundays, has a reputation around the city as sort of the Hard Rock Cafe of Irishness, which means that on St. Patrick's Day, which was tomorrow, the place is rotten with politicians and priests scarfing up the free boiled dinner, telling total crap stories about themselves and spending ten times the cost of the meal on gassy draft beers.

So what they do, to show their appreciation for the regulars like Terry, who eat their other three hundred and sixty-four suppers there every year, is they put out the free corned beef the night before St. Pat's. That way they can say thanks to their slushy, loyal clientele. That way they can protect their roots rep as a down and dirty neighborhood bar. That way they can get the heavyweights started drinking like maniacs twenty-four hours early. St. Patrick's Eve.

But why does he need me? Because I don't know why, I don't know, I don't, but for some reason St. Patrick's Day makes the people around here, even the not so warm and fuzzy ones like my brother, it makes them all gooey and clannish.

"Gotta have me boon 'round me," he said as he swept through the door after work. Which meant he was already drinking, on the job.

"How sweet," my mother said, about the boon business. She'd been drinking on the job that day too, cleaning the house. Now she and my old man were headed out to the Knights of Columbus, which is a Catholic club kind of like the Elks, only you drink your eyeballs out under a picture of the Sacred Heart instead of under a picture of the *PT-109*. They were going to tip back a couple of jars before heading to the night jobs—she the waitress, he the bartender at the O'Asis, which makes the Bloody look like the Ritz Bar. Then they'll have a couple more during and after work. Get the picture? So Ma finds this brotherly love stuff just lovely, and Dad thinks . . . well, to be honest, nobody in the world knows what Dad thinks. About anything.

"Piss off," Terry spat as they went out.

"Come home at a reasonable hour," Ma chirped.

"I won't bail you out," Dad said.

After Terry sent me to Irish up, I came back out wearing the rugby shirt with the four-inch-wide kelly green-and-white horizontal stripes, deeply wrinkled from life at the bottom of my closet.

"*There* ya go," he said as he jammed the hat low over my brow. Without even rolling my eyes toward it I knew what was up there on my head. It was a knit tam-o'-shanter, bright green like the underbelly of a baby tree frog, small brim with the cloth shamrock stuck on, and a baseball-sized white pompom on top. Supposed to symbolize, can you believe it, *pride*? I felt like a dink. Terry beamed at me from under an identical cap.

"Terry, you know, I'm really not much of a hat guy . . ."

He didn't even consider it. Threw his arm around me and squeezed so hard my shoulder blades touched. "Whatsa matter, you don't wanna look like me?" He laughed like he thought that was such an outrageous idea. "This is beautiful. Ain't this nice, Mick? You look like goddamn *me*. We could be goddamn twins, we could. They're gonna eat us up at the goddamn Bloody, boy."

He thinks we look exactly alike, but I don't quite see it. His hair is orange, and mine is, well, it's red.

But he was right, we lit the joint up when we walked in the bar. "Hey, he brought the Mick. Yo, boys, Terry brought the Mick along."

"'Course he did. Wouldn't be no St. Paddy's without no Micks."

They all smelled like cabbage already, Terry's buddies. The bartender drew a tall one for Terry before he even asked, and one for me too even though I'm exactly fifteen years old and look exactly fifteen years old. Terry tipped back and drank his beer halfway down, slammed the glass on the bar, then slapped me on the forehead because I wasn't drinking mine yet when for chrissake we'd been in the place for a minute and a half already. I drank, not as much as Terry drank in one gulp, because I don't have a blowhole in the top of my head, but I did okay. The taste was high and tinny, with a strong bitter finish, so I knew it was Harp.

The bartender slid two plates of steaming pink food across the bar. Terry growled at it like a ravenous happy dog. I covered my mouth and nose with my hands as the bitter, sulfuric odor of the cabbage climbed over me.

"Get it away, Terry," I said through my hands.

"What are you, crazy? This is some fine shit."

"That's exactly what it is, man. Get it away

from me or I'm gonna lunch all over the bar."

"You're embarrassing me," Terry said. "To-morrow people'll be steppin' on each other's faces to get this stuff. This is a damn honor, them gettin' it out for us tonight."

"*You* eat it, then."

"I would, but that ain't the point. You gotta eat it. Damn, this is CB&C, man, you ain't got no choice but ta love it. This is who you are. You can't not like it. Not in front of all my friends, anyway. Not tonight."

I shook my head, which might not have looked like much but under the circumstances was a pretty ballsy move. I knew how strongly Terry felt about crap like this, and he'd beaten hell out of me for a whole lot less.

He leaned close. "If I gotta cram it down your throat with a broom handle . . ."

I was very much afraid of my brother. Not just at that moment, but in general. However, I was even more afraid of the corned beef and cabbage.

"Kill me," I said.

He went all red, *redder,* that is, in the face. He looked over his shoulder at all his boys swallowing whole palm-sized slabs of meat. "Then just *pick* at it, for chrissake. I'll try to help ya without nobody seein'. Christ . . ."

I had truly humiliated him. So I did what I

could, spearing the tiny bits of bacon and onion that were cut up in the cabbage, making with the big chew like my mouth was full of a whole lot of bulk, washing down every bite with the Harp. Then I ordered Guinness.

"*That's* the boy," Terry said, ripping a sharp elbow into my ribs. "That *almost* redeems ya. Bartender, make it two."

The bartender smirked as he stared down into the thick brown head rising under the tap. "Right, Terry, like I was only gonna bring *one*."

No green beers on St. Patrick's Eve. That was for the dabblers tomorrow. Tonight was for red beers, amber ales, and especially, black beers. Stout. It was a liquid rainbow arcing around us as Terry's buddies finished their meals and gathered with their pints, always the big pint vases, pints of rusty Bass or Sam Adams, gold Foster's or Ballantine or, of course, old opaque Guinness. The common thread, of course, was the green shirt of whoever hovering behind each glass. I had drunk my Harp and my stout and had choked down my little bits of onion and bacon polluted by contact with the rest of the foul boiled mess, and I was teetering. Terry, trooper that he was, pounded down the drinks, *licked* his plate so clean that there was nothing left on it but his ever-sweet breath, and slyly polished off most of my meal without giving away our family shame. And feeling mighty proud of himself through it all.

"Any balls in the room?" Terry bleated, rubbing his full belly. "Who wants a game?" He pointed toward the tabletop hockey game with the big Plexiglas bubble over it, against the wall under the TV. Terry strutted over to the game, and six guys followed. When he took up his spot at the controls and looked up to see that I was still across the room, glued stupid to my stool, Terry came back and retrieved me, towing me by the shirt.

Terry played the first game and won, beating the fatter of the big fat Cormac brothers 6–0. That meant Fatter Cormac had to buy him a beer. It also meant, according to Terry's rules of order, Fatter had to buy me a beer. "No way, that ain't the rule," Fatter said. "Really, I don't need it," I said. Terry glowered. Fatter bought. I drank.

Danny stepped up and promptly beat the pants off Terry. "I quit," said Terry, which I don't even know what that was supposed to mean, quitting after the game was already over. I guess it meant he was quitting the loser-buys-the-beer part, since he didn't buy. Instead he slinked over to the little TV, the one with the Nintendo on it.

"You goin' to the parade tomorrow?" Augie asked from over Terry's shoulder.

Terry hit the pause button on the Nintendo basketball game, making the electronic musical tweedle-dee-ooo noise for pause. Terry turned around and threw Augie a disgusted look. "What kind of a ignorant question is that?" he said, then turned back to his game. Tweedle-dee-ooo.

It was sort of a dumb question because the thought of a St. Patrick's Day parade without Terry was like the thought of no parade at all—unthinkable. Augie knew that; he was just looking for fire.

"You goin'?" Augie asked me.

I shrugged. I shrugged because I hadn't thought much about whether or not I was going to the parade. I shrugged because I didn't much go in for any old parade crap anyhow. I shrugged because at that point, four pints full, I would have shrugged if Augie'd asked me what my name was. Anyhow, it wasn't a true question, with several possible answers. Not in this place it wasn't.

"Whatdya mean, ya don't know? Ya don't *know* if you're goin' to the parade? Where's ya goddamn pride, man? Y'know, this is the day, our day, every year when they bring the damn TV cameras down and we get to look into 'em and say yo and we get to see ourselves later on the news sayin' ya, that's right, we're still here, and this is who we are and the rest a ya can just chomp on my inky dinky pink thing. It's a important muthuh of a day."

"I guess so," I said. I didn't mean to sound like I didn't care about what Augie said. Augie, with his thick curly hair like black scrambled eggs falling over his low forehead, his acne-torn face, and his medication that kept him under control and that sometimes he didn't take, Augie was kind of frightening even though he was no bigger than me. So I didn't mean to sound like I didn't care about what he was saying, it was just that, well, I didn't care about what he was saying.

"You *guess* so?" he snapped. "You *guess*? You know, you young dudes just don't know, do you? Youse guys got no idea what's important. You got no sense a nothin' and that's what's goin' wrong wit' this no-balls chickenshit town."

I was so unhappy to be where I was, doing what I was doing. Everybody else seemed to be having such a great time. Terry was beating the video basketball game and talking trash to it. Fatter and Danny were pumping coins into the hockey game and saying the filthiest things to each other they could think of. One of Terry's other boys, the second round and ruddy blond Cormac brother, sat on a stool directly below the

TV mounted high on the wall, staring straight up at the Neighborhood Network News.

But I couldn't find a comfort zone. I was feeling too nasty to have any fun, but I wasn't quite gone enough to float above Augie's talking. Beers kept coming at me from I don't know where, and even though I already knew what a mistake it was, I kept accepting delivery.

"No sense a who you are," Augie said. "That's what you punks don't got today, Mick. Am I right, Terry?"

"Punk," Terry said robotically. "Punk. No sense a who he is."

"Who are you?" Augie demanded, very serious, taking Terry's support as a mandate to root me out.

I thought about the question, but I didn't think about it much.

"I don't know, Augie," I said. "Who are *you*?"

Was this all just a setup? Was he waiting for somebody to ask him and that's why he talked the way he talked? He lunged at me, tearing open his shirt, the pearly green buttons popping off and flying all over the place. "This is who I am, boy," he said, tapping himself on the chest. There, under the pointing finger, covering nearly his entire left pectoral muscle, was a tattoo. It looked just like the circular stamp of the Department of

Agriculture, faded blue block letters okaying food. It read USDA CERTIFIED PRIME 100% WHITE MEAT.

Augie leered at me. Nobody else reacted, having undoubtedly seen this all before.

"That's nice, Augie," I said. "In case you're in a car accident and they need to know what color you are."

"Ay," he said.

"Ay," I said.

"C'mere, check this out," Terry called, all excited.

Augie and I parked on either side of my brother's shoulders so that he could show us something he'd just discovered about Nintendo basketball after playing it a thousand times. "Watch what happens here," he said, pointing at a tiny black player in a green uniform. "See, when I press this button here what's supposed to happen is, the guy closest to the ball becomes the player with the brain, y'know, the one I control. But watch this." Terry pressed the button and as soon as the power switched to that player, to the one closest to the ball, the one with the black face, black arms and black legs, he turned white.

"Whoo-hee," Terry laughed as he and Augie rejoiced with high fives. "See that. Just when ya think everything's blowin' all to hell, somethin' comes along to restore your faith. See, even the slants at Nintendo understand that the black boys can play some ball, but it's the white guys that gotta make the decisions for 'em."

Terry was thrilled, like he'd discovered a great truth, a cure for something, found some key to the secrets of creation inside Nintendo's Double Dribble. He played harder, pressing his face almost against the screen, firing up three pointers, running up the score. Augie got all caught up in it too, rooting him on as rabidly as they all usually did for real sports events, which was *quite* rabidly. Augie bought three shots of Paddy. Terry clinked glasses with Augie and threw back his shot. Augie clinked glasses with me, even though my glass was just sitting there in the flat of my open palm as I stared blankly at it. "Gimme that," Terry said, and snatched the glass out of my hand, swallowing the contents down all in one motion. "You can't have that, you're just a kid."

"Here it is, here it is, here it is," Fatt Cormac called, bringing everybody to the news on TV. It was a feature on tomorrow's parade, but the screen was showing scenes from other parades, in San Francisco, in New York's Chinatown, from Mardi Gras in New Orleans, and from rights marches in D.C.

"What the hell is this?" Danny shouted, only to be shushed down.

The reporter on TV came on to interview first a member of the Cambodian Merchants Association, then the Gay Community News editor, and each discussed his group's excitement at marching in the parade.

"I thought they wasn't comin'!" Terry screamed.

Peanuts pinged off the television screen from every direction. The room filled with boos. A hot dog sailed like a missile, leaving a slash of mustard and ketchup on the glass. Someone threw a bottle that missed and lodged in the tight space between the TV and the ceiling.

"Cut the shit," Brendan the bartender yelled twice, first at the bottle thrower, then at the newswoman who came on to detail the court decision that had been passed down opening up the St. Patrick's Day parade to any group interested in participating.

Terry went berserk, standing on a bar stool and going nose to nose with the TV image. "Who the hell do you think you are, bitch, bustin' our time? This is *our* parade, muthuh. Who invited you all? Why don't you just go and have your own pissy little yellow faggot-ass parades and leave us alone!"

The place erupted with bottles, glasses, fists, and a few hard foreheads being banged on tables, chants of "Ter-ry, Ter-ry," and "Hell no, we won't go!"

"Oh, yes we will!" Terry yelled, turning to address the crowd from up on his perch. "Betchur Irish ass we're gonna be there, right, boys?"

My ears were ringing before all this started. They were screaming now, as everybody made as much noise as possible, including, I was surprised to realize, myself. I didn't know what anyone else was yelling, I didn't remember one single image from the news report that had just concluded, but my heart pumped and I watched my brother's power rising up there in the thick cigarette smoke near the ceiling.

Suddenly I was listening to myself whoo-whoo-whooping as loud as I could, as loud as anyone, yelling like cavemen must've yelled when they didn't know any words but needed to make noise just because everyone else was making noise.

Motherballs

Things tend to happen to me.

"What happened to you?" Sully was standing at the foot of my bed, wearing his navy pea coat and a Bruins cap. He was sipping a Coke.

"I'll give you a thousand dollars for that," I said.

He handed me the Coke. "Doesn't smell too good in here, Mick."

"Doesn't feel too good in here, either." I pointed at the spot between my eyeballs.

"Out playing with the big boys last night, were ya? Not good for your health, man."

"*Tell* me about it." I sat up slowly and drank

the Coke. "And why are you dressed that way?" He had high black rubber boots on, the buckles all jangling loose.

"What d'ya mean? It's for the snow, fool. You don't know it snowed all night?"

"Sully, when I say 'Tell me about it,' I *mean* tell me about it. Last night? What's last night? I remember being slung over Terry's shoulder like a sack of damn potatoes and all the way home looking at nothing but Terry's butt. I had a nightmare about it that lasted all night, so, thanks for waking me up."

Sully smiled and saluted.

"Well, what are you doing here?" I asked.

"The parade, of course. Ain't we goin' to the parade?"

I finished the Coke, making the loudest possible gurgling noises as I tried desperately to get more fluid out of the bottom of the cup. Then I collapsed back on the bed. "Maybe we'll just skip the parade this year. What're we gonna miss, a few pink-faced vets and fifty fools running for mayor?"

"Uh-uh, not this time. I hear there's some big stuff goin' on this year."

"I didn't hear that."

"What planet do you live on, anyway, Mick? I was just listenin' over at the Li'l Peach and everybody's talkin' about what you guys were stirrin' up last night at the Bloody. You were *there*, remember?"

I tried, to remember. I remembered excitement, enthusiasm. I remembered a lot of rah-rah stuff and people slapping each other's hands and hugging and pumping fists and I remembered Terry as some sort of charismatic leader and me getting a little bit of overflow glory from that, people buying me drinks, shaking my hand, me shaking back and hooting about it, the whole thing weaving together and blurring like a great barfly version love-in. What I did not remember was content. I hadn't a clue what anybody actually said, even though I seconded everything. Content, it seemed, wasn't the point anyway. It was the fire, was the thing.

"Sure," I said as Sully stood tapping his foot and looking at his watch, "I remember."

"Of course you do. Put your pants on and drink some Scope. We're outta here."

We walked the few blocks to the parade in the snow. It was tapering off now, light tiny flakes taking their time corkscrewing down onto our shoulders and hats, but there was already five inches on the ground. We walked up my street, where every house had a reminder of what day it was. Half the places had wind socks with shamrocks on them. The O'Donnells had a huge flag that said THE O'DONNELLS hanging from one flagpole mounted on the second-floor porch next to another, the orange-white-green Irish flag. Costello, the old bastard who turns off his lights at six o'clock on Halloween, who puts sugar in your gas tank if you park in front of his house more than once, who was arrested last year for killing a neighbor's dog by putting rat poison in his garbage—"proved the goddamn mutt was guilty though, didn't it?"—Costello had a banner tacked over his door in twelve-inch green letters: CEAD MILE FAILTE ("a hundred thousand welcomes").

"Top o' the mornin', boys," big Mrs. Donellen said to us as she shoveled out her car while big *Mr.* Donellen slept it off inside.

Sully tipped his cap to her. "Top o' the mornin'," he answered.

"If this is the top," I said when we'd turned the corner, "I'm in some deep shit."

"Eat some snow," Sully said.

"What?"

"Really. Eat some big mouthfuls of snow real fast. Your head freezes and you feel better."

I scooped up two handfuls of snow and swallowed them down as quickly as I could. For ten seconds, miraculously, I felt better. For ten seconds.

Then my headache returned, with three of its friends. "Thanks, Sul," I said through a Clint Eastwood squint.

"Don't mention it," he laughed, fully aware.

We turned onto Centre Street, walked on past Prince Edward Avenue and Labrador Terrace, streets just like mine. Then we hit Sycamore, a long street cutting through the neighborhood, that was at one time the heart of the neighborhood. These days, though, there were as many empty lots as there were triple-deckers, many houses boarded up, many others just empty. FOR RENT signs appeared in almost every first- and second-floor apartment window, and FOR SALE signs on nearly every lawn. There were a handful of old Irish families still living on Sycamore, but they tended to be the meanest, most defensive, most offensive people in the whole neighborhood. New families moved in on Sycamore all the time, but they didn't look anything like the pale old families. Sully's parents and grandparents started out on Sycamore, as did mine, but Sycamore Street today stood more as the dividing line after which the streets no longer look like my street.

Sully can be old-fashioned sometimes, like the old folks who look at Sycamore as sort of the Old Country. "Just look at it," he said, shaking his head sadly as we passed. "It's like they don't even know it's a holiday down there."

I had to laugh at him. *"Holiday*, Sul? What, are people supposed to be partying in the street for *Evacuation Day*? So George Washington drove the Brits out of Boston. I mean, thanks, George, but let's get over it already."

He waved me off. "Evacuation Day is just the excuse, you know that. The day off is for St. Pat's, and you'd think people would appreciate it. That friggin' street used to *buzz*, boy."

He was right about one thing, the street was quiet. A couple of people shoveling, a couple more underneath an old Toyota Corona jacked up with no wheels and Jesus face stencils on the headlights. The four legs sticking out from under the car, twisting and kicking with the effort of removing some twenty-year-old corroded brake lines, made angels in the snow, like we used to do when we were little.

I guess we were staring, me at my angels, Sully at his ancestors, because we started getting looks. The black man in the driveway of the house closest to us, the house Sully's mother grew up in, stopped cleaning off his car, leaned on his broom, and glared. I nudged Sully and we left.

"See what I mean?" Sully said. "It's just so

hostile. Used to be that we could hang on that corner all day if we felt like it."

"We were gawking," I said. "We wouldn't like it if he did it to us."

"Bullshit. Used to be able to gawk the hell out of that street and nobody minded. If that guy wanted to come over to my street and gawk awhile, I wouldn't mind at all. As long as he went home after he was through."

I put my arm around him. "He *is* home, Sully. He lives two streets away from you. In your mother's house."

He threw my arm off of his shoulder. "That ain't funny," he said.

"Change, man," I said.

"It's too quick," he said.

"So?"

"And too close."

"Aha . . ."

"Aha, what?"

"Afraid?"

"I ain't no racist," Sully assured me. "I mean it. That ain't what this is about."

"What's it about, then?"

"It's like, y'know how them rappers Public Enemy have that disc talkin' about 'Fear of a Black Planet'? Well, I ain't got that. It wouldn't matter to me if ninety percent of the earth went black, and I couldn't travel to any of them places without getting killed. 'Cause then I would just stay home where I belong. So I ain't got no fear of a black planet. What I got is a fear of a black Sycamore Street."

I had never thought about it like that before. But as soon as he said it, I knew what he meant. Sycamore *was* getting to be a scary place, a foreign place, when not too long ago it was *our* place. And it sure was awfully close to home.

But being scared and being ignorant don't have to be the same thing. They don't.

They don't.

"Know what I mean?" he asked.

"No. I don't know what you mean." We were approaching the parade route, could hear bagpipes, Sycamore Street was far enough behind us to be unreal again. "I ain't afraid of nothin'," I said, which Sully found pretty amusing.

We wound our way around, looking for people we knew, which was pointless since we knew just about everybody at the St. Patrick's Day parade. We were supposed to meet Baba, who said we'd be able to spot him by his GOD MADE THE IRISH #1 sweatshirt. Probably ninety-five percent of the crowd had that same sweatshirt on, with their coats spread wide open to the cold to show them off.

"Yo, Bones," Baba called out, and we went to him. He had already found Terry and his friends, and all were sitting on a prime piece of curb a quarter mile from the start of the parade. They were all drinking long neck Budweisers, bar bottles, from a case Terry was sitting on. They were eating hard-boiled eggs. People were packed elbow to elbow at all good curbside locations, but nobody was within ten feet of these guys.

"Oh my god," Sully said, pinching his nose shut.

Terry walked right up to me with an egg in his hand and punched me in the stomach, meaning he liked me. "Mornin', boyo," he said. "Have a egg."

He was stuffing it in my mouth already by the time I wrestled it out of his hand. "No thanks," I said, and automatically flipped the egg to Baba, who ate it whole without shelling it. Baba would have eaten dung if they threw it at him. To impress them. Baba's dream was to be, in seven or eight years, just like Terry and Augie, only bigger and stupider and more dangerous. He was being groomed for the position.

"Well, have a beer, then," he said, ripping a cap off a bottle with his teeth. "Courtesy of our sponsor," he said, referring to Bloody Sundays, who had supplied not only the beer but the eggs.

A shopping bag filled with cartons of eggs.

I gagged. All I could do was shake my head.

Terry threw me a disgusted look. "Just as I was starting to have some hope for ya."

"Don't be so hard on the kid," Danny said from his cross-legged perch on the ground. "I think we seen some potential in the boy last night."

"Was that last night?" Augie said. "Feels like it was just yesterday."

"Or this mornin'," Terry said, and they all yukked it up. Sully looked at me. I shrugged. I still didn't get it. Baba didn't get it either, but he wanted to. He took a long drink from a curved pocket flask and called for another beer. He had the right idea, if what he wanted was to get closer to the boys. I realized as I scanned the group, cock-eyed and bleary and reeking a million reeks beyond the boiled nasty stench of last night, that they hadn't gone home, they'd stayed in the bar until coming here.

"What *about* last night?" I asked, which made them howl. "No, I'm not kidding, what about last night?"

"You're a hoot, kid," Fatt Cormac said, balancing an egg on the mouth of a bottle before chugging it all down together. "When your big brother there finally gets himself killed—which could be any time now—you're gonna take right over. Hell, you're ready already, stuff you were sayin'."

"What? What, *what* did I say?" It was no use. The more I asked, the more everybody laughed at me and said things like, oh, you crazy shit, and get outta town and stuff like that that made me feel worse. This was beyond embarrassing, forgetting the things I said, it was frightening. Not only did I not know, but whatever it was it was making me into a sort of hero to *Terry's friends*.

"Ya, and they almost didn't let me back in after I took you home, ya little bastard," Terry said, smiling, menacing at the same time.

One of the Cormacs went to crack an egg, but when he knocked it against his knee the whole runny mess slimed down his pants leg. They only had a dozen cooked eggs—the rest were raw.

Like the opening volley in a World War I battle, thirty snare drums started snapping in the distance, opening the parade. With one crazed voice, the whoop of joy flew the length of the route, making my head gong, but my heart thrum, as I screamed along.

It must be the drums. The drums that overwhelm you at the spearhead of the parade, that change things so completely that your own heart adjusts its beat to be in step. Patriotism. What the hell is that, patriotism? It's in a drum. When the drums play, thirty at a time, I am a patriot. Or an acrobat, or a clown, when the circus comes to town and they get off the train for the elephant walk from South Station to the Garden and somebody beats and beats on those big drums and I forget about how bored and disappointed I am when I actually attend the circus. For the elephant walk I'm there, I'm juggling, I'm marching, I'm roaring, ready to pack up for clown college, because those drums do it, with that primal whatever it is, those drums make me feel like I *belong* to something when usually I don't belong to anything, and I'm stupid with whatever it is they want me to feel.

Just like the St. Pat's thing. The drums were beating for St. Pat and so there I was, like it or not, no matter what I thought about who I was yesterday or tomorrow, for that drums-beating-cold moment I was Mick, a mick, The Mick. It started with the fife-and-drum corps and if you can't get all excited for the fifes and drums, then what are you? We were primed. Sully was clapping his hands raw with, I think, a tear in his eye. Terry screamed a rebel yell and of course his boys joined in, as the music subsided a bit, and the musicians were followed by the vets. World War I guys, the remaining six of them, all dignity and solemnity as they refused to wave, or smile, or focus, they stood at attention on the back of a flatbed truck passing at a crawl.

"Good Jesus God love ya, men," cried a fifty-ish woman cheering from the opposite side of the street.

The World War II and Korea guys followed right behind, walking too fast, to prove that they didn't yet need to ride the flatbed. A little less somber, a little more cocky, and a lot more drunk than the older soldiers, every one of them waved and pointed at somebody, because they were all somebody's father and somebody's grandfather.

"Uniform's lookin' a little tight there, Dad," called a voice right behind me.

"I got a *gun,* boy," answered the long tall marcher with the massive bulge under his shirt. He laughed and aimed the gun at his son, who must have been perched like an apple on my head. I ducked.

The Vietnam guys. The spooky part of the parade. They were the ones who always wore only part of the uniform. Fatigue pants with a white T-shirt. Olive drab shirt and cutoff dungarees. Beret decorated with medals over white karate pajamas. Every year lately, the Viet vets got a little more popular, the cheers increasing, their waves finally answering, but still, I thought the feeling in the crowd was more scared and anxious than anything else.

And the worst part, for them, was that they now came right ahead of the veterans of Desert Storm. First, it felt kind of funny to call them veterans since these were the same kids who still hung around the middle school playground and drank beer all Saturday night with the teenagers. And the other thing was, the ovation was *so* intense that I think it pissed off both the Vietnam and World War II guys, who turned and pretended to open fire, joking without laughing.

The Boy Scouts. The Girl Scouts. "Gimme a cookie," Terry yelled, shocking the little girl who was walking close by, sending her crying the rest of the march. The Mulcahey School, Irish step dancers, came stomping, jigging, and hornpiping their way by. "No jiggs, no jiggs," Baba screamed, getting big laughs from both sides of the street.

There was a bit of calm as the Franklin School for the Disabled walked and wheeled by displaying their artwork. Papier-mâché dogs that looked like sheep, a painting of green. A nine-leaf clover. Terry and his friends shut up and drank, which was their sort of tribute. There was polite clapping all around. The *God love 'ems* were muttered *everywhere* in the crowd, but nobody shouted anything. The snow had stopped, but there was still plenty on the ground, making for a surreal, silent padding march. The boys drank harder, swallowing at a trot now, lining up the empties not in their slots in the case, but neatly along the curb. By the time the neighborhood youth soccer league quick-stepped by, knobby knees knocking in their short pants uniforms, the parade had no sound to it. The wait was on.

It didn't take long. Behind a street-wide banner came the group representing the new largest block of merchants in the area, also the second largest fishing operation and moving up fast. The Cambodians. For paraders, they were awfully unsmiling. They had reason to be.

The first noticeable thing was the nothingness. No clapping, no booing, only silent footfalls in the snow. But it was tense. The feeling seemed to be *please just get through so we can be done with this.* But then somebody clapped. Deep in the crowd on the opposite side of the street. A second person joined in, a third, then a few more but that was it. Nobody near us tried it.

"Cut the shit over there," Terry hollered at the clappers.

The leader of the Cambodian Merchants

Association, the man from the newscast, acknowledged the support, smiled, waved, and said, "Thank you." Several others behind him also waved, an odd sight with a whole section of a parade focusing its attention on a small group of a half dozen, craning to see, to thank them, deep in the crowd.

"You shut your yellow hole too," Terry yelled, pointing at the man.

The merchant turned our way. "I won't," he said clearly, evenly. He hadn't yet closed his mouth behind the words when a snowball splattered in his face. The man stood still, the parade stopped behind him, and he wiped his eyes with the end of his scarf. He started walking again and was hit again, harder, with a motherball, the kind the Kellys on my street like to make, the kind they pack tight and dip in water to be left outside overnight stacked in pyramids like cannonballs to freeze into rocks. It sounded like a punch in the mouth with four school rings when the motherball hit his face.

The man doubled over, covered up, when the snowballs started flying everywhere. The woman behind him screamed, ran to him and they huddled together. Terry was standing on top of the beer case to get better leverage as he fired down on the Cambodians, throwing snowballs, ice-balls, whatever was handed up to him by two ten-year-old boys working slavishly by his sides. The fat Cormac brothers were too drunk and lazy to even rise, just sat there on the curbstone packing and hurling snow high into the air to rain down like mortar fire. Danny merely drank, nodded, scanned, like Patton observing a battlefield, pleased.

"Move along, move along," said the policeman in charge of the detail. He and the rest of his men, who had all volunteered to work the parade for free, mostly just waved the marchers along without getting too close to them. "Okay, come on, you guys, cut it out now," the sergeant said to the boys, like it was a mere prank rather than an assault that now involved fifty percent of the spectators.

Slowly, the parade did move again. "Good ruck, mucklucks," Augie spat as they moved away.

"Here," Terry screamed as he lobbed an egg. "Make some egg foo yung outta this." The egg smacked directly into the back of the head of one of the last Cambodian marchers, but he didn't stop or turn or slow down as the clingy raw egg ran down his neck, under the collar of his shirt.

The next group along, lagging notably behind, was the Neighborhood Society, headed by the city councillor from the district, who waved brainlessly, smiled, pointed at every individual like he was a long-lost friend. But his vision was strictly peripheral, as he refused to look straight ahead at the limping group not thirty yards ahead.

"Sharkskin," Terry called, using the councillor's neighborhood handle.

"*There* he is," Sharkskin called, pointing at Terry. "There's the boy." Then, pointing at the bottle in Terry's hand, Sharkskin motioned for Terry to bring him one. Terry rushed to the open-top convertible Le Baron and handed over the bottle, which Sharkskin raised high to a thunderous ovation. He took a long swallow, then motioned Terry toward him. "Lookin' like goddamn downtown Saigon around here, ain't it?" asked the councillor, who had fought hard against the opening up of the parade. "I was thinking of bringing them Nam vet loonies back here to wipe 'em all out."

Terry rushed back to tell us all about it. Of course the boys cheered and toasted the good old Shark. Baba, notorious for his inability to control his temper, his mouth, or his liquor, was out cold facedown on the sidewalk. Sully looked at me. "This ain't quite as much fun as I thought it would be," he said.

I looked away from him, looking everywhere, for some sense, for something that made sense to me. My head hurt worse and worse. "Sure ain't much of a *celebration,* is it?" I asked Sully, as low as I could. He shook his head.

"What the fuck are we doin', Sul?"

"We're not doin' nothin'. We're just standin'. We're clean."

I shook my head, and shook it more. "Are we, though? I don't know. I mean, I really don't. Are we clean?"

Sully shrugged.

The bagpipes, convoluted and weaving, somehow unearthing a tune and looking around for something better at the same time, welled up slow and soothed a lot of the stuff. A lone piper, in a kilt of blue and green tartan with a matching cap and high socks, had a section of the parade all to himself. He floated through like high clouds, like a thick slow breeze, quieting everyone, humming us all to sleep and brushing away everything that came before him. Bad weather, anger, dissonant chords, dissonant people, were no longer a part of the day, as he left nothing but honey in his wake.

But that too was swept away when the end of the parade came up. The Irish-American Gay Pride Coalition marched along, in numbers that matched any other group, under a banner raised high on ten-foot aluminum poles. The crowd in our area had swelled with people who had finished marching and doubled back to where everyone knew the action was going to be. There wasn't even a hesitation this time.

Little boys were scraping their fingernails on the pavement to get up every speck of snow to throw. Every ball seemed to be a motherball, maybe just because of the ferocity of the throws, but the street became a war zone.

"Screw, this ain't no St. Pansie's Day parade. Get them faggot asses outta here." Terry had quickly switched from snowballs to eggs, then from throwing them to running right up and jamming them in people's faces.

"Youse is all lyin' anyway, 'cause there ain't no Irish faggots," Danny proclaimed to several shouts of "Damn right!"

I was frozen, my hands at my sides. "Let's get the hell out of here," Sully said, grabbing my arm. But I was transfixed, watching it all. "Come on!" Sully yelled.

Suddenly Augie appeared right in our faces. He stuck an egg in my hand. "What are you two doin' standin' around wit ya thumbs up ya asses for? Throw this."

I stared at the egg in my hand.

"Here," Augie said, trying to put the other egg in Sully's hand.

"I don't want that," Sully said.

"You better want it." Augie lifted Sully's hand, placed the egg in the palm, and forced his fingers closed around it. He then whirled around, pointed to a group of the Cambodians who had drifted back to the other side of the street, and said, "There ya go. Now throw it."

Sully coolly looked into Augie's vacant blue eyes, and went into an imitation of Muhammad Ali. "I ain't got no quarrel with no Viet Cong," he said, and dropped the egg to the sidewalk to splatter both of their feet.

Augie was incensed, at the voice as much as what was said. He balled a big fist and stuck it in Sully's face, asking the big question again as he showed off his other tattoo, the green lettered WITE across his knuckles. "Are you forgettin' who you are?"

Sully didn't answer, which finally made Augie maddest yet. Augie then drew back his fist, behind his ear, to pound Sully. But just as he was about to let it fly, I reached out and grabbed the fist. When Augie paused, stunned, Sully bolted. He's got a good heart, Sul, but not a very stout one.

Augie turned on me. "You got balls, boy. So much I'm thinkin' about breakin' your head. But

I won't." He lunged, gripped my shoulders, and spun me around to face the other side of the street. "Throw the sonofabitch."

I balked.

"Throw it or I'll kill ya. And don't think your brother'll stop me."

I was looking straight into the mayhem. The street was filled with Terry and Danny and the Cormacs and a few freelancers pushing and spitting and slapping marchers, who covered up or ran or swung madly back at them. But mostly the scene was filled with a lot of people watching and doing nothing. Like me. Until now.

"Throw the muthuh," Augie said from over my shoulder, and as he said it, he clamped down on my earlobe with his teeth. "I'll rip it right off," he garbled.

I only hesitated for a second, and he bit. First, a little pressure. Then a pinch. I squinted, gritted through the pain. I felt a tearing as he bit and pulled the ear away from my head at the same time.

I threw the egg. I threw it over everything, into the harbor, probably, I threw it so far over everyone. Augie chomped and I felt the blood. "People are gonna think you're a stray from the Gay Irish-Americans," I said, and he yanked his head so violently I thought I was going to lose the ear. He pulled another egg out of his jacket pocket and placed it in my hand.

I threw this one for real, as the clamp on my ear made my eyes tear. I watched the trajectory, its gentle arc as it crossed the road, sank, and landed dead in the face of the Cambodian woman who had earlier wrapped herself around her husband after the motherball. She stood like a statue as her friends made a fuss around her. Her husband turned and lovingly wiped the egg away from her face with that same scarf, picked pieces of shell off her coat.

Augie let go of me, lingered long enough to chuckle like the devil in my ear, then joined the fray.

I felt the tears in my eyes spill over as my ear burned and I watched the scene play out. There was a lot of chatter in the Cambodian group. I started making my way over there, feeling a need to get to the woman and do I don't know what—to undo the humiliation I knew couldn't be undone? But I was going. As I hit the street, I saw the leader, the woman's husband, leaning to listen to a white man, a friend of my parents, who was pointing me out. In a flash, the Cambodian man locked on to me and came running my way. I wasn't going to fight him no matter what, so I just held my hands up and yelled "Wait, wait," but he steamed my way anyhow.

I was going to let him. I prepared to be bowled over, closed my eyes and stood. But it never happened. When I opened my eyes, Terry and the man were wailing each other, going toe to toe, the man giving as good as he got while crying tears of rage. Until two of the good old cops came over, one grabbing the Cambodian man from behind in a bear hug, pinning his arms to his sides, the other grabbing Terry in a similar way, only holding him by the waist, leaving his hands free to hammer off two and three and four more unanswered shots to the man's purple, bloody nose.

The sound of sirens from the distance of every direction broke things up quickly. Terry knew that the police on the way to the scene now would be different, not as sympathetic as the St. Patrick's volunteers. As soon as the officer let him loose, he booked, followed by the boys. As he ran he grabbed me by the arm, yanking me, my wheels spinning under me just fast enough to keep me from falling on my face, as I ran along out of blind stupid instinct.

What'd I Say?

How does news travel the way it does? When we ran, we ran of course to Bloody Sundays. It didn't take us any time to get there, Terry rushing back to the place all flushed and giggling like a little boy bringing home his first perfect spelling test crushed in his hand. Still, word beat us to the bar.

"On the house, on the house, on the house, on the house, on the house," Brendan the bartender called, shooting each of us with his finger gun as we strode through the door. The annual corned beef and cabbage and green beer and bullshit crowd was gathered inside already, one big sweaty blob of people pressed from wall to window, from bar rail to door. The odor was ten times as strong as it had been the night before, that and the ten thousand back slaps I got on my way in nearly drove me to the floor.

Which would have been fine, actually. I would have just lain there the way smart people do when there's a fire, letting the smoke and noxious fumes float over them, the flames lap away everybody else. I would keep my nose pressed against the dusty floor, my arms covering my head, and then in a while I'd get up and walk calmly out, stepping over all the dead bodies. No such luck though. They wouldn't let me go down.

"Here, here, c'mere, boy, here, have this." Some old duffer I recognized but didn't know was jamming a slab of corned beef between a couple of slices of Wonder bread that had some meat-juice stains around the crust. "Here ya go. They're all outta the free dinners, a-course, but here, you take this." The meat kept wiggling out of the bread, and the old guy kept wedging it back in with his cracked, brown-speckled, sclerotic hands, then waving it all in my face again.

"No, really," I said, turning my head ninety degrees and closing one stung eye. "I want you to keep it."

He didn't hear me, or wouldn't accept it, because once again, the sandwich was in my face. "Here, son, have this, you earned it."

"I don't *want* it," I screamed, drawing some looks, making the old man stare down into his plate and mumble. "Sorry," I said, patting him on the shoulder. He brightened, tried to talk to me. I walked away. A spot opened up at the bar and I snatched it. As soon as I took up my spot on the stool, Terry was there.

"You could give up that seat," Terry said to the man next to me, one of the part-time, green beer, St. Patrick's Day rent-a-micks. The man hopped right off the stool.

"So, whadja think? Fun, or what?" Terry said to me as Brendan slammed two cold ones down in front of us. I pushed mine away.

"Get this out of here, man," I said.

Brendan pushed it back. "Get outta town. You're a hero. Drink the beer."

People are always trying to force me to swallow things. "I'm not a damn hero," I said, and before I could slide the beer away again, Terry grabbed it.

"He's right, he ain't a damn hero," he said. "He's just an apprentice. *I'm* a hero."

"That you are, boy," said Tommy Coughlin, an off-duty firefighter who draped both big hands over Terry's shoulders. "You're the man,

Terry, preserver of the faith, keeper of the flame, righter of all things—"

"Shut up, Tommy," Brendan laughed. "Go home to the wife."

"Don't stop him now," Terry said. "I think he's soundin' pretty good. Just a little full a the old blarney today, that's all he is."

"Full a the old *barley*, ya mean," Tommy said, laughing, exchanging fist smashes with Terry. "But no shit, man, y'know, I ain't no prejudiced, you know that, but what you guys done today, that was right, it was the right thing."

"Preserved the purity of the day, is what ya done," said Mrs. Doherty, a sixty-year-old semi-widow with her husband, Jim, slumped at a table across the room. "Now I ain't no bigot, mind ya, but them people had no business in our parade. You fellas did the decent thing." She slapped me hard on the back, nearly sending me into the cheap bottom-shelf booze. The admiring crowd gathered in a semicircle around us. Terry loved it, swinging all the way around to survey his flock from the pulpit, leaning back with his elbows on the bar. I held my face in my hands, looking into the yellow mirror with the fake marbled squiggle all through it behind the bar.

Up on the big TV, cable access was playing the annual St. Patrick's political breakfast, where the dwarfy needlenose president of the state legislature sings lame sappy Irish ballads and ridicules everybody who has a real job. It's like a TV Mass around here, but this time Terry had the senator beat for attention.

The Milkman came over to solemnly shake Terry's hand. They call him the Milkman because he is, actually a milkman. Drives a silly truck painted like a Jersey cow for his father until he inherits the little empire himself. "I deliver to some a them people, y'know, Terry, and, well," he shook his head grimly, disgustedly, "well, you know what I'm talking about."

Terry nodded, nodded, soaked it up, winked, and let the Milkman kiss his ring before clearing out. The band started warming up. My god, the *band*. Please, not the band. Had it been a year already? This is the thing people wind up talking about most when the gas clears from another March 17. The band is a three-piece outfit made up of a drummer with only a snare drum; his wife, a versatile instrumentalist who alternates between tin whistle and accordion; and on vocals, *every* pipefitter and bookkeeper with inhibitions quelled enough and strength raised enough to grip a microphone. The three stand on a makeshift stage in the front window that takes up the space of two round cocktail tables, making for big fun every year when three or four soloists end their sets by plunging accidentally into the crowd.

The first singer, a priest new to the parish, tore right into "My Wild Irish Rose." The earnestness. That's what I could kill them for. The earnestness. The senator was up on the TV screen screeching the same song at the same time as if it was some kind of bozo celebrity lip synch contest. Same heartfelt squints, same sour notes.

"Brendan, man, you got a couple of Advil for me?"

Brendan slid me another beer.

"No, no, no, I don't want another beer, I want something for my *head*."

Brendan slid me a shot of Jameson. And the copy of Brendan Behan's *Borstal Boy* that was always on display right beside it.

I didn't try to talk to Brendan anymore. Talk got harder anyway as the caterwaul grew louder all around us.

"Semper friggin' fi!" Borderline Bob screamed in Terry's face. They called him that because he was, even by local standards, psychotic. He was pointing at the inscription tattooed on his large, heavily veined biceps. "Semper friggin' fidelis," which is *exactly* how it read. "Always friggin' faithful. That's me, Terry, man. That's my motto.

It was the motto when I was in the corps, and it's even on my family's goddamn coat of arms, if you can believe that." Which I couldn't, because old Bob's not exactly *semper fi* with the truth. "But today, man, it's you, Terry. You're the faithful one. You are the true one. Y'know, I wish I could tear this sucker right off myself, and I would, I'd rip it right off and I'd stick it right onto you 'cause you're the guy that deserves it." And with that, Borderline Bob began what appeared to be a sincere effort to claw the tattoo right off his own arm.

"Hey, I appreciate the thought, Bob, but could you maybe do that over there," Terry said, motioning toward the corner by the one brick wall in the place.

"Sure. A-course," Bob said as he headed off in that direction, scratching, scratching, picking, as if he were just trying to lift a postage stamp off an envelope. "I love you, Terry, man. I love you," he muttered, then, as he passed me, "Hi, Mickey."

"Hi, Bob."

"I ain't no racist," Marion said as he shook Terry's hand. Marion, with his mother behind him, nodding. Marion lived with his mother and not with his father, who went out for a quick cold one twenty years ago and never came back. Marion Junior was named after his father and not after his mother, who was named Marian by some freak of luck that they just made worse by dumping the name on the kid and giving him probably the full set of nervous acne he still has at age twenty-five. "I ain't no racist, Terry," Marion Junior said.

"He ain't," Marian said, and the two passed along to me, shaking *my* hand in what had become a sort of receiving line.

"I'm workin' for the Edison now, y'know," Marion said. "Anything you need, you just let me know."

"They *had* it coming though, didn't they?" Marian said to me. I thought to answer, couldn't, shrugged instead. "Ah but you understand that, I know, after all what you said the other night."

"What did I *say*?" I begged, taking her hand in mine.

"Oh you're a divil, just like my Marion. And you know what else, you're a throwback. I ain't heard words like you used in decades. Nobody says *jungle bunny* no more. Nobody says *jigga-boo* or *chinky*—"

"I *fuckin'* did not say—" I snapped.

"Y'know, boy," she prattled on, "it was just the way we talked in them days, so everyone knew who everyone was. Now, with them all breathin' right over our shoulders instead of stayin' where they belong, we can't say the words we want. But you—"

"Me, nothin', all right. That wasn't me. You know, you drink a little too much, and your memory's a little screwed."

This made Marian chuckle. She pulled her hand out of mine and threw me a wink. "Don't you worry, now," she said. "We know how to take care of our own."

Marian's words shoved me further into sickness, the vile taste coming back up out of my belly again. Did I need taking care of now? I was not one of their own, goddamn it.

And there was no way, even drunk, even in that atmosphere, that I could have said those things.

I was pretty sure.

"Go have a drink, Marian," I spat, wanting her and her words out of my space.

She took my words as encouragement, and went off to find that drink.

A cheer rose up as the local entry in the up-coming mayor's race bought a round for every-body in the place. Not one of the once-a-year bums, this man was in the Bloody four or five nights a week. The difference was that he was buying, this one time. He knew how many miles he could get for his beer buck, guaranteeing the votes of the sloppy, soggy clientele for a one dollar draft on the one day it would work. The man stood across the room and raised his glass slyly to Terry, not risking the political jeopardy of sitting with him.

Another priest—where do they all come from, and why do they all want to sing?—stood on the stage. Slyly, again slyly, always slyly, he nodded and winked at Terry before revving up a ferocious, dissonant "Wild Colonial Boy." Augie ran up to Terry and they exchanged warm, excited head butts. Terry drank my drinks, Augie's drink, everybody's drink, held both fists high in the air, and roared. He was king, and he knew it.

"Where are the Cormacs?" Terry asked.

"Workin'. Holidays they gotta go in second shift, so they took off already to pick up their truck." The Cormacs work for the phone company. "Said they'd be back in a while."

The chunky Maguffin sisters mounted the stage, blocking out the musicians behind them. Singing to their combined families of thirteen kids, they squawked a "McNamara's Band" so aggressive the people up close—people who can stand quite a lot of abuse or they wouldn't be sitting there—scooted their chairs backward, and Brendan yelled "You suck, get off the stage!" Their children, all of them blond as new baseballs, laughed their little devil laughs, munched onion rings and buffalo wings in their too-small, mismatched polyester sweat suits. The sisters didn't hear, sang blithely on with the same conviction and confidence as everybody else.

"Where's Baba?" Terry asked.

"Cormacs carried him home," Angie said, "dropped him on his porch."

The two laughed and butted each other again, as hard as they could. Blood rolled down from the middle of Terry's forehead, between his eyes, over the crooked nose, turned, ran out along the deep crease beside his lip and chin, lined them like the mouth of a ventriloquist's dummy. He never noticed.

I couldn't look at him. I couldn't look at anybody else in the place either. I turned my face once more to the mirror behind the bar. To myself. I couldn't look at him either. I took the latest of the beers Brendan was pushing on me, and I drank it.

I watched in the mirror as the one woman in the place nobody was talking to stood, ambled stiffly to the stage, patted her bouffant, sucked her brown cigarette, and sang "My Wild Irish Rose." Had she not heard it earlier? All three times? Did she not care? Why should she, since nobody else seemed to. Tears fell, bodies swayed.

She got a rousing ovation. I was about to heave.

"Hey champ," Augie said low into my bit ear. "Havin' a good time? Bein' the big man? Feels good, don't it? We'll turn you inta somethin' useful yet."

"Get away from me, Augie," I said.

"Sure I will, little boy. You had a big day, I understand. But listen, you tell that little Sullivan ratty friend a yours that I'm lookin' ta have a little chat with his ass." As he backed away, Augie pinged my ear.

"Hey brother, what happened to your ear?" It wasn't my actual brother who asked, but Danny. Terry and the boys like to call each other *brother*, especially at sloppy times like this.

"An animal bit me," I said.

"Oh, that's too bad," he said, genuinely concerned, but not stimulated enough to inquire any further.

"Y'know, I'm not prejudiced, but . . ." I heard a deep voice say to Terry.

"Nah, neither am I," Terry could barely choke the words out through the laughter, his own, then the other man's. I heard the slapping of palms.

"Hey, hey, hey, hey, everybody shut up!" Brendan yelled. He flicked a switch and killed the power to the microphone into which Augie's grandmother was squealing "Take Me Home to Mayo," while Augie yelled "We love ya, Grammy." A few bars later, she stopped. Brendan aimed the remote at the TV and cranked the volume. The reporter, the same one from the night before, was describing the "chaos" and "savagery" of the parade. The bar patrons, most of whom had only heard about it until now, watched the videotape.

Again, for the camera, Terry charged into the Gay Pride group. Again, the Cormacs threw eggs. Again, Terry yelled obscenities. Then, in the background, out of the anonymity of the crowd, again I threw an egg. Then another, as Augie seemed to merely hover behind me.

And again, in close-up, Terry hammered away at the Cambodian man who had charged for no apparent reason into the fray.

Like a heavyweight championship fight that would be playing on that very same bar screen, the crowd went berserk, punching the air, ducking, duking, cheering the video Terry on to victory.

By the time it ended I had my face deep in my hands, my elbows propped on the bar. The pounding on Terry's back sounded like timpani.

"Hey," he said when it subsided. I parted my hands enough to peek out at the ocean of beer before us. There had to be forty full pints. Gifts. I took one. I didn't feel like accepting it, I didn't feel like drinking it, but I sure as hell felt like having it stroking my brain.

"What happened to your ear?" Terry said, finally noticing.

"Sonofabitch clipped me," I said.

"Ay," he said, and clinked my glass with his. He was thrilled.

"Ay," I said dead, and drank lively.

"And what happened to *me*?" Terry laughed, seeing the head butt blood in the mirror. I figured it was a rhetorical question, so I didn't bother telling him. I just stared at the two of us in the marbly mirror—Terry scarred and bloody and ugly and drinking and smiling at the same time so that the beer ran out of the corners of his mouth, me scarred and bloody and drinking and not smiling. I didn't look like him, goddamn it, him with his orange hair and me with my red. I looked out beyond us, at these people, my people, as they say. I could have done something right there. I could have done something to my brother. I stared and stared at his stupid reflection, and a little at mine, but mostly his, and I could have done something to him. The more I stared, the more I was going to do it. All it would take now was one tiny push, like if somebody got up and sang "If You're Irish, Come into the Parlor," that would do it. First I'd puke, then I'd strangle my brother.

Good thing I never had to. When the cops tromped in, the place went silent. The sea of bodies—very much like a body of liquid by this time—parted reluctantly. Everybody knew where the boys were headed. Everybody but Terry, who was so gone by the time they tapped him on the shoulder he kept drinking even though he could see them in the mirror.

"Boooo," came the first lone voice. Then everyone else. "Boooooo." Everyone booed the cops, who laughed, covered their ears, waved it off.

"Come on, Terry," the lead cop said. "We have to take you. You're on video, for god's sake."

"Can I finish my drink first?" Terry said.

"Of course. We're not inhuman."

Terry leaned way over to one side, to show them the mother lode he was working on. "I'll be with ya in about six hours," he said.

The cop smiled, took Terry by the arm, and they went peacefully. The booing slurred into one sound like a barn full of cows.

"Jesus, you people," the cop said. "It ain't like we never arrested him before. We'll try to have him back before closing time." The booing and mooing stopped.

Terry's crooked grin widened, his legend growing with every unsteady stride. Somewhere deep in the crowd, somebody started whistling the song from *The Great Escape*, from the scene when the Nazi guards were leading Steve McQueen back to solitary confinement and another prisoner threw him his baseball glove.

When they were gone, the tin whistle rose up slowly, serenely, and the snare drum rolled. Marion Junior climbed the stage and started singing with Marian at his feet. Could it be? "Wild Colonial Boy"? Again? Only this time it was like a dirge instead of the usual romp. In tribute to Terry.

Danny leaned into me. "I guess you're in charge now, bro," he said.

I got off my stool and started digging my way through the room. Somebody spoke to me, I didn't even know who because I didn't look.

"Brother, y'know, I'm no racist, but—"

"It's a good thing there are no racists around here," I said, "or things could've gotten ugly today, huh."

The guy thought it was a joke, and a pretty good one as he turned and repeated it to the group behind him. I pushed on past.

When I reached the stage, I tapped Marian on the shoulder, asking her to excuse me. Then I grabbed her son by the ankles and shook him, nearly taking the legs out from under him.

"Shut up!" I yelled. "Would you stop already? Just shut the hell up. Stop singing the same stupid damn songs over and over. Move on, for chrissake."

He stopped singing. Everybody stared like there was something terribly wrong with *me* as I walked out and "Wild Irish Rose" started up again.

Part Two

♣

What Have You Done,
My Blue-Eyed Son?

"**Y**o, men."

Funny how life doesn't change for Baba. He could kill a person on a Saturday and still he'd be waiting on his porch Monday morning to say "Yo, men," and catch the bus to school with Sully and me. Then, while we waited for the bus he would still do his stupid trick of the day or tell his disgusting joke of the day, before mentioning that oh by the way I offed a guy over the weekend, if he thought to mention it at all.

"Yo, watch this," he said as he leaned against the bus stop sign, hung his head, and let a long, clingy spit hang down.

"Ugh, god," I said and started to turn away. But he made that urgent grunting noise the way people do in movies when they're tied and gagged and are trying to say something important. So, I looked, fool that I am.

The spit dropped lower, and lower, somehow still holding together, until it hung six inches from the pavement. He paused for a second, let it swing a bit, then he snapped it up, sucking the whole thing all the way back into his mouth like a great string of spaghetti.

Sully just stared at him blankly. He was kind of shocky this morning. We all were kind of shocky, except for Baba, who was kind of Baba this morning.

I started to say something, choked, tried again. "You're an animal, Baba," I said. "Not just because you can do stuff like that, but because you actually spend *time*, thinking *up* stuff like that."

"Oh ya? What kind of animal am I?"

"A pig, I guess. Ya, like a big giant razorback warthog pig, only with an even smaller brain."

"Hey, Bones, you got a feelin' like you wanna be dead this mornin' or somethin'?"

"No, I got a feelin' like maybe I wanna start associating with a better class of creature, that's the kind of feeling I got."

"Oh what, you a better class a creature than me now?"

I hesitated, but only to make it look good. It didn't take a lot of thought. "Hell yes."

"Gargle my balls, pal," Baba said, grabbing his crotch and yanking it in my direction.

"Well, I stand corrected then, don't I?" I said, warming up pretty quickly to the superiority idea.

"Well, Bones, y'know you standin' here makin' y'self out somethin' better than me, like you're so different than me, when my old man got a videotape at home from the news that says you ain't nothin' like that at all."

"Screw, Baba. All right? I ain't nothing like you, you ain't nothing like me, and that's all there is to it." I turned my back to him, watched down the street for the bus.

Baba grabbed my shoulder from behind with one big powerful paw and spun me around with a jerk. He smiled mean as always and smarter than usual in my face.

"Y'know, I heard a million guys like you talk this trash before, this 'I'm better than you' shit."

"No, not guys like me."

"*Exactly* like you. And you know what else? They're all still here. Still just like me. Just like you."

How crazy was I? How well was Baba getting under my skin? I pushed him. Put both of my hands on his car hood of a chest, and tried to move all twelve tons of him. He didn't move. I moved. As I pressed my hands into him and shoved, my feet skidded backward and I slipped off the curb into the gutter.

"Ouch," he laughed in my face. "Please, no more, no more."

It was useless, obviously. Sully snapped out of his trance long enough to shake his head no, telling me to simply let it go. So I did, sort of. I looked away again, down the block to where the bus was now in sight. That was all I wanted, just to get on the bus, let Baba go all the way to the back like we always do, and then not go with him. To be done with him. But that would have been the smart thing, so of course it was out of the question. My mouth wasn't quite finished yet. I had to add a real snotty, "You ain't worth my time, pal."

"Oh, you're so tough, Bones. I guess I'm just lucky I ain't no four-foot-tall gook chick or you'd really be showin' me what a man you are."

He shrunk me. As I stood in the gutter I felt like the curb was up to my chin, like the red-faced little rat I was. The bus pulled up, the door opened right in front of me. Instead of getting on, I turned, walked up to Baba—who leered at me—and took a wild poke at him. Before I could hit him, he reached out and seized me by the throat, squeezing, lifting me up on my toes.

"So you're feelin' a little crazy right now for some stupid goddamn reason," he said, almost friendly. "Don't go riskin' y'life over somethin' that's gonna pass away like a hangover." Then he threw me at the bus, saying as I stumbled aboard with Sully's help, "That one's for free, Bones. Don't be expectin' no more of it."

I *was* crazy. Baba hadn't done anything to me actually, but I was focused on him, on what he was, and what I decided I *wasn't*. We used to be the same—that was the problem, and that was bothering me more and more. So maybe I just figured if I could get Baba to murder me, that would separate us. I'd be somehow purified.

Baba did sit by himself in the back, while Sully and I shared a double near the front. I stared out the window, feeling the welts rising on my neck from Baba's grip. I looked at Sully, who was also staring at the red marks, shaking his head. We didn't say anything the whole way to school.

As I got off the bus, I was greeted. Sitting on the bench at the school stop were five seniors from the school, Asian guys, two down on the seat, three up on the seatback. I didn't know any of them since, being a sophomore, there was no reason they would ever have talked to me before. But they sure wanted to talk to me now.

"Saw your show on the TV the other night," said the one everybody knows as Mr. Quan, the leader. "You looked good."

"Photogenic," said one from behind.

"Athletic," said another.

"You might have a career in the pictures," Mr. Quan said.

I had frozen in the bus doorway when they first started talking to me. Now with people barking at me to get out of the way, Sully gave me a little shove. As I stumbled off the bottom step, Mr. Quan rose and stood on the bench, staring knives right into my eyes.

"Deep shit," Sully whispered.

I couldn't believe what was happening. What was this? I never had any trouble with any other kind of people before. Of course I never talked to or hung out with any either, but that was okay, that was the trade, wasn't it? We just all leave each other alone and everybody's cool, right? I never expected this.

"What do they want with me?" I said, playing stupid with Sully and with myself.

If My Fist Clenches, Crack It Open

Baba never, at any time in his life, knew anything about anything that was worth knowing, so how was it that he knew my life was going to get so hard?

The month following the whole St. Patrick's mess lasted about six years.

The Asian guys eventually caught up to me.

I found a letter *inside my lunch bag inside my locked locker,* that said "Yum yum, this tuna sandwich is going to taste extra special good now," and even though it seemed like nothing was done to the food, who the hell could eat it after that?

I think six people in the school made eye contact with me all month, and those six I had

"Unfortunately, I think you're famous, man."

That didn't sink in right away. Then it did. "Oh my god . . ."

Just as I was about to explain to them about the mistake, about what a fine guy full of goodness I actually was, they moved. They all stood, the lower-tier guys standing on the seat, the upper tiers standing high above. Then they came down, the front row hopping down to the sidewalk and the back row filling their spots at exactly the same time. These boys had the sonofabitch *choreographed.* I was intimidated enough to squirt myself, but just a couple of drops.

But I wasn't goin' nowhere. Uh-uh, couldn't do that no matter how wrong they were about me. Can't run, can't say, "Let's be reasonable about this." You just can't. I don't *know* why you can't, so don't ask me. It's just that the operation doesn't run that way. Sully understood it too, standing there beside me looking as mean as he could, which wasn't a whole hell of a lot of mean, but it was a nice gesture anyway. We'd take our lumps together.

Then the miracle thing. Just like a movie scene run backward, all five guys hopped right back into their original positions on the bench.

Were we tough or what? Without turning, I looked at Sully out of the corner of my eye and saw him looking back at me.

"We ain't got no beef with you, O'Reilly," Mr. Quan said, tough but nervous at the same time. Baba had just stepped off the bus, last as usual.

Baba didn't say a word, just stood hulking, arms folded across his chest, above and behind Sully and me. Mr. Quan stared, mostly at me, with blanching glances at Baba. Baba didn't move. The Asian guys didn't move. Sully and I certainly didn't move—if Baba'd had a pouch like a kangaroo, we'd have been inside it.

Mr. Quan tried once more. "We ain't got no beef with you, O'Reilly."

"Sure you do," Baba said coolly.

That was it. Mr. Quan and his boys made a decent show of it by hanging around for another minute or so, but as soon as Baba spoke, they were already packing. Unless they could round up another twelve guys, they weren't going to play with Baba.

He waited for them to be completely cleared out before Baba split from us too.

"Not such a bad thing, to have a animal around sometimes, huh, boys?" he said smugly.

I started to thank him, but he waved me off. "Another freebie. You was pretty fortunate today, Bones, but don't even bother to [...] wanna wish ya luck wit' the rest of y[...] 'cause you're gonna need it."

He walked away, and I knew I wo[...] Baba standing behind me ever again[...] scary. But that was good. Right?

fights with. To see me was to punch me.

Sully got mono from, I think, fretting for my life and, by association, his own. This kept him home for three weeks, reducing my support at school by roughly one hundred percent.

My father revived his dream of buying the O'Asis. He's never owned anything. Not the shack we live in, not a car, not a dog, not a bicycle. But every time the O'Asis comes up for sale—every six months or so—he thinks he can own a bar.

Terry got out of jail and threw himself a restraining order–burning party.

And I think I fell in love.

The month truly bit.

The place I had to go to every day was school, and the last place I wanted to go to was school. April, May, June, then out. I didn't think I could make it. Starting with April Fool's Day, it got harder and harder to haul myself out in the morning. Some mornings I just never did.

One morning I was sitting at the breakfast table five minutes before the start of homeroom. Dipping my toast into the yolk of my greasy, bubbly, over-easy egg, yellowing up the toast, then not eating any of it. Terry sat across from me like usual, both hands wrapped around a triple-size mug of black coffee, shaking as he tried to guide it to his mouth.

"You're going to be late, Mick," Ma said as she tromped down into the cellar with a mound of washing.

"I'm not going," I said.

"Terry, drive your brother to school," she said, "so he's not late."

"No, no, no, *no*," I said. "I'm leaving, I'm out the door. No need to do that, Terry. I'm gone. Bye."

Terry stood up, guzzled the coffee. "A-course I'll drive ya. Don't be a ass."

He would have run me over with his truck if I said no, so I got in. A beautiful thing, Terry's pickup, '69 fat red Ford with the big rounded hood and big spaces in the floor to watch the street whiz by.

"Havin' some trouble at school, are ya?" Terry said as he revved the tired engine.

"Ya, I guess."

"I know how ya feel. I didn't like school much either when I was your age."

My age? He didn't like it much when he was six, when he got booted out for the first time for smashing the fish tank.

"Here, this'll help," he said, and pulled a six-pack ring out from under his seat. There was one beer left clinging to it. "It's only a Lite, but it'll do for mornin' time."

I popped it right open, the fine spray misting my face. I took a long suck on the can. Terry reached across me, pulled a pint of Wild Turkey out of the glove compartment.

We didn't talk, which I appreciated. I finished the beer, and was filled with it. I didn't normally do this, the A.M. snort, because it had a bad effect that at first felt like a good one. That first cool blast of morning. The okay thing, the jingling belly, the quick bink in the head, the momentary silliness that made everything that was hard and nasty about my life or anyone else's seem stupid. It was a blast but it was only a blast, gone just as quickly as the last swallow of backwash in the bottom of the can and I was left with the rest of the day, and the rest of the day was just a ball rolling down a steep hill and I wasn't ever going to catch it. Not again, not after the first cool blast.

I threw the can into the bed of the truck, a hook shot out the window. I stuck the empty hand out toward Terry and he filled it with the pint.

It wasn't a pleasant ride, Terry jerking the truck into gear when it didn't want to go, then racing it to the next set of lights where he had to slam on the brakes again. Stop signs were not a problem, because he didn't stop. Except once.

There was an elderly woman waiting at the intersection to cross. One of those old-timey elderlies who make a big deal out of it every time they go out. She had on a suit, dark pink jacket and long matching skirt, white gloves, a small shiny pocketbook, and a sort of cylinder-shaped white hat with a spray of baby's breath poking out of it. I could smell her lilac perfume all the way from there. I guess it was her celebration of the arrival of spring. And, by the way, she was a black woman.

Terry muttered "What restraining order? What two hundred yards? Truck ain't got no restraining order," and charged toward the intersection. Ten feet short of the crosswalk, he screamed on the brakes, making the frail woman drop her bag, even though she was a prudent five feet back from the curb. She picked it up and Terry motioned her with a broad sweep of his hand to cross the street. The woman nodded thank you and started slowly across. When she was right in front of the truck—in his sights, he said—he blasted the engine, making it roar to catch her notice. The woman froze, staring at the ground, trembling like a wet dog.

"Cut the shit, Terry," I said.

He grinned, leaned out the window, "Sorry,

ma'am, the thing just races every once in a while. It's old. You know how it is."

She didn't look up, instead tried to toddle a little quicker across. Terry, looking more insane than usual, said, "Three points, boy. Too bad she wasn't younger and pregnant, that'd be ten points." And he dropped it into gear.

"No!" I screamed, but he was already into it. He put his foot on the gas, boosting the truck ahead, right into the woman, then screeched the brakes with the bumper six inches from her hip.

The woman doubled over, covering her face with her hands, crying. Her purse fell, her hat toppled off her head.

"You asshole," I said as Terry sat there watching her, giggling.

"Oh, be a man for chrissake, will ya, Mick?"

I looked away from him and back at the woman, who was still in front of the truck, petrified, going nowhere. I thought, she just wants to be left alone. She doesn't do nothing to nobody. She just wants to cross the street. To get home in time for *The Price Is Right.* She just wants to go to the mall in a van with the other old folks once a month and buy tiny portions of food and put a little extra sugar in her tea and make sandwiches with only one chewy slice of ham in them and to be left in peace. And y'know, she was helpless, and why couldn't he just leave her alone?

But that was it, wasn't it? It was the helplessness that he loved and that he hated, the helplessness that made him horny.

I looked back at Terry, all smugness and cowardice, and for that moment, I wasn't afraid of him.

"C'mon, lady, move along," he said. "I got places ta go."

"Hey, bro," I said, and when he turned, I took the pint bottle and racked it right off his forehead.

I jumped out my door and went to the woman. I heard Terry slam his door and figured I was in for a beating, but I didn't care. I picked up the hat and the purse and took the woman by the arm to the sidewalk. Then I turned, ready to meet Terry. But he wasn't there. He was piling back into his truck and peeling out, pointing a menacing finger at me and scowling under a puffing pink brow. I looked down the block and saw the policeman walking our way. Which certainly explained Terry's shyness.

"I'm fine, officer," the woman said. "I was being harassed by some hoodlum in a truck, but fortunately this decent young gentleman happened by."

Decent young gentleman? I hadn't exactly been swimming in *that* stuff lately. This I could like. And she didn't even know I was in the truck with Terry.

"Good work, son," the cop said, then looked quizzical. He leaned a little closer to sniff me.

I pulled away, turned my face from him. The last thing I needed was for the officer to smell what really made the hero brave. So much for basking in my new goodness. "You okay now?" I asked the woman, and when she said she was I took off. "Can't be late for school," I said in a rushed voice, like I cared.

I was very late for school, which earned me detention, so I could be very late after school too. But I felt good. I had done something okay. My brother wasn't going to slit my throat for another nine hours or so, so that was cool. This was already a good day by recent standards.

But there was nobody to tell it to. I was at school.

Well, there was one somebody I'd have loved to tell, except she'd never listen. Her name was Evelyn. Evelyn was special. She was in the avant garde of hating me, having hated me long before I was on TV. I asked her to go to a dance with me one time and she ripped three buttons off my shirt without even saying no.

She was so cold to me, it was thrilling.

And if there was an opposite of me, an anti-me, it would be Evelyn. She was a poet. She was Cuban. She also said she was part Naragansett Indian and part Russian. She had long silky black hair that came down to her waist some days and disappeared completely under a hat on other days. Nobody ever knew how much of what she said was true, because in fact she was weird like you'd figure a poet would be. But some days she did look like a real Indian, and some days like a real Russian. What she always managed, though, was to look like nobody else in this brain-dead school. Being so different meant she was largely considered to be out of her mind, thus she had almost as many friends around here as I did. So now and then I figured I had a shot with her.

Evelyn was in detention with me that day because instead of the essay on Oscar Wilde she was supposed to do, she handed in a poem: "All in the gutter/some look at stars/while others try to lure/students into their cars." As usual nobody knew what she meant, but the English teacher, Mr. Wolman, seemed to take it rather personally, getting all red-faced and tearing the paper into fifty million pieces.

So Evelyn was down there in the gutter with me, sitting right next to me, and I was feeling a little bit of okay with myself, enough to give her a try.

I pulled my mini magnetic backgammon set out of my inside jacket pocket. "Wanna play?" I asked.

She turned a fish eye on me. "Roses are red/violets are blue/ . . . screw," she said.

"Why are you so mean to me?" I asked.

"Because you're a pig."

"I am not a pig."

"Yes you are. Stop talkin' to her." The voice came from the other side of the room.

"What's your problem, man?" I asked.

"Just leave her alone or I'm gonna kick your ass."

Here we go round the goddamn mulberry bush. Again. "Eat shit," I said, but I didn't enjoy saying it as much as I used to. I was getting like one of them oldies acts that sing the same songs, do the same dances a million times until it's all meaningless. You know the tune by now.

"Oh ya?"

"Ya."

"Lick my pinga."

"Lick your . . . ? Well, lick mine too."

"Outside?"

"Damn right outside."

And it was a date. Evelyn showed up to

watch, bless her frigid soul. So did four of the eight other detainees. And, of course, me and Ruben Cruz.

"Your breath stinks, you Irish mick stupid drunk bastard."

It was probably true, since he said it from three feet away.

"Stay away from my sister," he said, walking toward me.

"Okay," I said. "How 'bout your mother?"

I was lying on my back, listening to the cheers before I could even raise a fist. "Hit him, Cruz, man, hit him!" Cruz obliged, dropping crisp shots to my chin and temple before I managed to roll him over. When I was sitting on his chest, I returned the favor, holding his collar bunched in my right hand and pounding him in the mouth, smack, smack, smack, three times, all mouth, shake those teeth loose, show a lot of blood, always the way.

I was hitting him almost at will, *winning,* as I do in about twenty-five percent of my fights. But it didn't feel good. Even as we both scrambled to our feet and went on punching—I snuck up a nice fiery breadbasket uppercut that made him suck out loud, he popped an overhand square into my cheekbone—the cheering went on. "Hit him, Cruz! Drop him! Kill him." And I listened to it. I didn't used to listen to it. It was always just noise before, same for everybody who fought. Just noise.

But this time I heard it, and I couldn't hold up anymore. I passed up a clean shot at Cruz's face, grabbed him by the hair, and threw him down. I didn't jump on him. I backed away. I was through.

Cruz got up and came after me. Drilled me with a straight right to the jaw. He waited for my reaction with his fists raised. There was no reaction. "Pig," he said, and punched me again, in the mouth, making those bottom teeth wiggle.

First there was a gasp from the spectators, then nothing. Cruz was perplexed, looking at everybody else for some sign, but there were no more calls for my head, then back at me. "Freakin' pig," he spat, then turned and walked away. He wasn't talking about my interest in Evelyn, because he didn't care. He didn't even look at her before stalking off.

She came up to me as the crowd slithered away. She smiled, a friendly small smile I hadn't seen before. "That was stupid," she said.

"He's your brother?" I asked as I blotted my lip with a Kleenex. "I've never even seen you talk to each other."

"He doesn't like me very much. He's just

been waiting for a reason to beat on you." She shrugged, waved, and left.

So there it was, back again, my great day. I felt so good, watching Evelyn walk away with those long graceful strides that seemed to make her float rather than step, her shiny braid wagging at me like a big playful monkey finger, come here, it was telling me, or no, no, no, but either way it was sweet play.

I made up my mind I wasn't going to fight anyone, ever, over anything, again.

As I walked through the door at home, Terry brained me with a kitchen chair, knocking me cold.

Toy

"**I**'ll play with you."

The guy was answering a question I'd asked four days ago. A question I'd asked somebody *else*. He was that kind of guy.

"Huh?"

"I said I'll play with you if she won't. I love backgammon."

His name was Toy. He was in detention when I was. He was also in detention when I wasn't. He was always in detention. Not because he was a bad guy; there wasn't a disagreeable thing about him. But for being a little on the loony side. That stuff, oddness, pe*cul*iarity they call it, that's what drives 'em mad around here and the loons are always winding up in the jug for mostly nothing. They used to lock Toy up all the time for his hat. He wore this kind of straw Georgia cowboy hat with the sides scooped up and the front brim bent way low over his face. The no-eye guy, people called him, and you had to crouch low, crane your neck, look straight up at him if you wanted to look him in the eye. He'd let you contort yourself up like that too, rather than tip his head back to let you see him.

He still wore the hat almost all the time, even in gym which could be pretty funny with his sweats on and running around trying to decapitate somebody in dodge ball. But the teachers got used to the hat or just quit because they didn't jug him for it anymore. They just jugged him for every other damn thing.

"You still have it on you? The backgammon game?"

"Ya, I got it," I said, still in shock over being spoken to on school property by somebody without his hands around my neck.

"Well, whip it out then."

We were in study period, in the library. All I was doing was all I ever did during study, which was stare at Evelyn as she read big volumes of poetry, slammed the book shut, stared at the ceiling, sighed, sometimes cried, went and got another book. I found myself, like when you're watching a fight or a basketball game on TV and you can't help ducking and juking along, pantomiming the action—doing the things she did, staring up to the ceiling, sighing, folding my hands prayerlike the way she did. When she cried . . . well, okay, I didn't cry, but I did feel bad for her.

"Sure, why not," I said, opening the game.

"Ya, why not," Toy said, "It's not like she's ever going to acknowledge you or anything. After the game you can go back to mooning and moping."

"Shut up," I said, but I laughed anyway. "And she *did* finally talk to me. After the fight."

"Oh, I'm sorry. What did she say?"

"She said I was stupid. Then she left."

"Well, say now, that's a whole nother thing I didn't know. You got a *relationship*."

"I'm getting there," I said.

"No you're not," he said as he set up the board.

"And why not?"

"Because you're a well-known pig, that's why not. And that young lady is a person of principles. *And,*" he shook the dice and tumbled them out, "she's not a Caucasian." He looked up at me, but not all the way up. His hat stared at me.

"I'm not a pig," I snapped, drawing looks from

all over the library. "And you better shut up."

The hat laughed at me. "I've seen you in action. I'm not worried. Roll the dice."

"Well, if I'm such a pig, what are you doing talking to me?"

"Because I think there's more to it. I know that, while you certainly have strong piggish qualities, you're not really a total pig. You don't have the heart for it."

"Gee, thanks. I feel so much better about myself now." I rolled the dice, got a two and a one.

Toy rolled double sixes. Rolled again, got a three and a one, started blocking my guys in. "And despite what the whole world seems to know about you, I kind of think they might have the story wrong."

He looked so sure of himself, so sly, smiling without looking up from the board.

It hit me. "You know!" I said. "You know. How do you know?"

"I'm smart."

"You're not *that* smart."

"I saw where the first egg landed."

"You were there!"

"And I saw that guy chewing on the side of your head, whispering the sweet somethings in your ear. And I saw you walking toward the lady you hit."

I started shaking Toy's hand furiously. I felt like I'd been rescued from a shipwreck. Somebody in the outside world knew, or at least suspected, that I wasn't an animal like my brother. "Thank god," I said. "Thank god. Sanity."

The word struck him funny. He pointed at himself. "Sanity?" he said.

"Wait now. What were you doing at the St. Pat's parade? You ain't Irish."

"That I ain't," he said. "Actually, I'm Cambodian."

I hesitated, even though I was stunned. Until I realized he had to be kidding me. "Funny, you don't look Cambodian," I said.

"Goes to show," he said, smirking. "You just never can tell."

"Oh, I don't know about—"

"Game's over," Toy cut in.

I looked at the board. It was a total devastation. I never made it across the fifty-yard line.

"You have some kind of unslakable thirst for absorbing beatings, huh?"

"Apparently I do," I said.

Monday morning Sully returned from the mono.

"So what happened while I was away?"

The fat lip Cruz gave me was gone, but the

lump I got from Terry and the chair, long and thick like a finger running between the skin and bone on my forehead, was still prominent.

"Nothing," I said.

"Cool. For you, I'd say nothing happening was a good thing."

"Oh, wait a minute. Now that you mention it, a couple of things did happen. I got beat up by five Asian guys, one Cuban, and one psychotic brother. I rescued an old black lady from the foaming jaws of Terry. I fell in love. And I made a new friend at school."

Sully looked at me for a few long suspicious seconds. "Bullshit," he said. "You didn't make no friends."

"I did. I'll show you."

Loitering in front of the corner store across from the school was Toy. He was sitting on a plastic milk crate, a long skinny cherry-smelling cigar sticking out from under the hat. There was about an inch between the brim and the ash.

"Hey, pig, how ya doin', man?" Toy asked. I loved it.

"Him?" Sully said, gesturing with his thumb. "You made one damn friend, and it's *him*?"

"So what's wrong with me?" Toy said, all cool, letting the cigar smoke just eke out of his nostrils, gather under the brim of his hat, then roll up over the edges.

"You're a bigger loser than *he* is, that's what," Sully said, turning the big thumb on me now.

"Thanks, Sul," I said.

"Listen, I'm sorry. I didn't mean you weren't fine guys. It's just that, well, you're like zits, probably harmless but who the hell wants to be seen with ya."

Toy went into aggressive ignore-Sully mode. He stuck the cigar into his mouth and let it hang while he talked around it.

"I've been thinking about your lady problem over the weekend. The way to Evelyn is—"

"Whoa, whoa," Sully jumped in. "Evelyn, Mick? Did I have mono, or friggin' malaria? Evelyn is the great love you fell into?"

"Ya, what about it?"

"About it is this. Of all the many thousands of people who hate your guts, there is nobody who hates them more profoundly than Evelyn does. So unless I'm confused on exactly what the purpose of loving a girl is . . ."

"She's softening."

"She's *softening*, is she? You use a blowtorch, did ya?"

I turned to Toy. I had allowed myself to forget

how futile this was. Sully was back to remind me. "I don't know what I'm tryin' to prove. Sully's right, I don't have a prayer."

"Of course I'm right," Sully said, satisfied. "Don't waste your time. Go out and find a chick who lives a hundred miles away and don't know anything about you. Then you got a shot. Evelyn, she ain't your type anyway."

"What is it he should object to, Sullivan? Her exquisite beauty or her keen intelligence?" Toy asked.

Sully looked at me, dropped his chin and gave me the deadpan eyes. "Who is this guy? He needs some slaps, I think. You need some slaps there, pal."

"Slap me," Toy said.

Sully waved his hand at me like he was demanding money. "Okay, how many slaps we got in petty cash, Mick?"

I was looking over Sully's shoulder, down the street. "Uh-oh," I said. "Speaking of slaps, Sul, did I forget to tell you that Augie was looking for you?"

The sound of Augie's name made Sully shut up and look in my eyes. "Ya, you forgot to tell me that little thing." And when he saw the way I was looking off, what little bit of color he had drained from his face.

"What are you now, *better* than the rest of us, Sullivan, you little rat muthuh?"

Augie had spun Sully around so they were face to face, with me right behind Sul, who was stone frozen.

"What you been, hidin'? Makin' me come lookin' around f'you for weeks."

"I . . . been sick," Sully said in a small, whimpering kind of voice you usually use on someone who might have a little sympathy. This was the wrong place for it. "I had mononucleosis, Augie."

"Shut up, I don't care what you had. I took that as a personal insult, what you didn't do there at the parade." Augie started prodding Sully hard with his finger, poking him with every sentence, pushing him backward. "You can't throw one measly egg?" Poke. "You forgettin' who you are?" Poke. He'd now driven Sully back into me and with one finger was poking us both down the sidewalk. "Your *buddy* there can throw a egg. How come *you* can't throw a egg? Ain't got no quarrel with no Viet Cong, huh, smartass? I think maybe you ain't got no quarrel with the Irish faggot Americans either."

Like the flick of a blade, there was Toy, slicing his way into the sliver of space between Sully and Augie. He'd gone unnoticed, sitting there on the crate, leaning against the storefront. But as soon as he got in there, Augie started his retreat.

"What the hell do you want?" Augie asked.

Toy didn't say a word. The only sound was the click of his square-toe boots on the pavement, taking one step forward for every one Augie took backward.

"What, Toy, you gonna kill me? You gonna cut me?" Augie said nervously, badly pretending those thoughts didn't bother him. "C'mon, I ain't afraid a you," he said, almost jogging backward.

How come I didn't know Toy was that big? He looked now so big, big hands, long legs, square but meaty shoulders. *Raw boned* is what they'd call him if he was an athlete.

Sully and I stood on the sidewalk staring, enraptured, still pressed together like Augie had us. "C'mon," Augie yelled from a distance, "I'll kick your ass. C'mon." When the distance between them reached three blocks, Toy stopped following, walked back to where we were. "I'll kick your ass," Augie's tiny, distant voice called.

When Toy was back, bigger now somehow, sort of hovering over the two of us, and us smaller and stupider than usual, we just stared at him for a few seconds.

"Okay, I won't slap you this time," Sully said.

"You know Augie, I take it," I said. "Or at least he knows you."

"We better get in," Toy said, letting the gone-out cigar fall from his lips. "They're gonna jug me again if I'm late. I can't have 'em jugging me anymore."

Welcome to the Hotel Toxic

What was funny about the whole Sully-Toy thing was the way they refused to quite warm up to each other, but wouldn't back away either. They always seemed to be jockeying over something, like whether or not Evelyn and me together was a good idea.

"Think about it," Sully said, wagging a very serious finger. "If she really is part Indian, with the Mick here being, well we all know what he is, do you suppose their offspring would be unusually *thirsty* little buggers?" Such remarks—the kind Sully made all the time—caused Toy to go stone cold, but we always eventually got past it.

And more and more the three of us spent our discretionary time around school together, with even Sully realizing that being in Toy's presence was not too bad a place to be.

"Where do you live, Toy?" Sully asked as we sat on the school steps one afternoon.

"At home," Toy said.

"Very good. But where is that?" We had no idea where Toy was from. Most afternoons we'd hang around in front of school or over at the store for a while, then Toy would go his way and we'd go ours. Not that I thought about it too much, but really we didn't know anything about Toy. That was okay by me because I didn't feel like I needed much. Not Sully, though. He needed much. These things are important to Sul.

"Why do you need to know?" Toy asked. "What does it matter where I live?"

I started to figure Toy lived someplace crappy. Crappier even than where we lived. "Back off, Sul," I said.

"No," Toy insisted, "that's okay. But I want to know, what does stuff like that matter to you?"

Sully got fidgety, kicking at the steps as he talked, pacing some, tossing pebbles like three pointers into the trash barrel. He likes asking questions a whole lot more than answering them. "I don't know. It's just, regular stuff, y'know, background stuff. A guy likes to know things about another guy. You know."

"No, I don't know. Why does a guy like to know things about another guy?" Toy sometimes could tie you up with his blank voice, his Store-24-clerk I-don't-get-it way of talking. Some of it was real, some of it acting, but all of it was killing Sully.

"Dammit, Toy, you know what I mean. Like, 'Toy,' I mean, what kind of a name is that? Where does it come from? What are you? What are your parents? Y'know?"

Sully fidgeted faster and faster. The deeper he sank into this thing he was digging, the more he squirmed. Toy sat calmly, hunched, his elbows on his knees, his hands folded in front of his chin. Sully swam like a fish in a tank in front of him. Slowly, Toy started nodding.

"You do. You do understand," Sully was thrilled to say.

Toy continued nodding. "No," he said.

"Maybe this is a good time to go," Sully said, clapping his hands and yanking me up from my spot beside Toy. We started walking, and Toy sat. I didn't say anything because for the first time all day Sully was right, it was a good time to leave because I thought I could feel Toy tensing up. Something I didn't think any of us wanted.

We'd gone about twenty feet down the side-walk when Toy called us back.

"What's up?" I asked when we were back standing in front of him.

"Ya, come on now, come on now, Toy, we're pretty busy guys here, places to go, things to do." I don't know what Sully was expecting, but he was definitely in no hurry to reengage Toy.

"You want to see it?" Toy asked.

"Nah, thanks anyway," Sully said, though he had no idea what the subject was.

"See what, Toy?" I asked.

"Where I live. You want to come? I could show it to you."

He almost stuttered it out, he was so bad at this. He was apparently not used to inviting people over, which was okay enough since we weren't used to being invited.

And gone was the nervous, bumbling Sul. He was on this like a rat. "Absolutely, man, we'd love to," he said. Because when it comes to a person's personals, his vital statistics, Sully is one curious cat.

We walked, tagging like baby ducks behind Toy as he led us to the places on the far side of the school, where we never go. To the stuff we never see. All our times are spent normally traveling the distance between home and school, and back, no need to make much use of the area east of the wrought-iron school-yard fence. There was just nothing there. We either played at home, the region around Sycamore that no longer included Sycamore, or we went into town, taking the train to zoom through all this on the other side of the school without ever looking at it because, like I said, there's nothing there.

But the checkerboard squares, spoking out of either side of Centre Street, looked a lot like it did on my side. We walked through the black section, closest to the school, past two play-grounds filled to capacity with kids and throb-bing music and adult guys in basketball games where somebody crashed hard into the chain-link fence every ten seconds. There was food cooking somewhere, something spicy and ricey, and every time I'd smell it I'd hear laughs and West Indian accents.

He took us past the small Southeast Asian community, which was like a wall of silence thrown up against the buzz of the nearest streets and I wanted to hurry through because I felt like everybody still recognized me from you-know-what and they were all quiet because they were plotting something special for me.

The cars. The Dominican-Cuban-Puerto Rican

neighborhood blew me away with the love of their cars that looked to me like something out of Daytona and Indianapolis. I think half the cars were opened up, jacked into the sky, guts half spilled onto the sidewalk, and for every Toyota and Mazda and Chevy there were three men laboring to bring it back to life while their kids played soccer in the street between them.

We didn't know how many worlds, like Mario Brothers, Toy was going to take us through, until we came to the end of the end of the world. It's what people around here, at least the people who talk in front of me, which of course means the Bloody's kind of people, it's what they call No Man's Land. It was where the so-called mongrels of the city wound up when they landed here. Transients. Sicko life-stylers. Newer waves of non-English-speaking immigrants like Russians and Slavs with no community in place and other folks who just weren't looking for any damn community.

It was a working waterfront, on the edge of a canal, skinny houses sandwiched between frozen fish packing plants and big produce wholesalers. Why was it that all you could smell were the *bad* fish, and the *bad* vegetables? Where the city just dropped into the bay or the bay dumped into the city and travelers legal or not jumped off boats and said, "This is it, this is home now," settling into one of the million roachy rental units within a spit of the pier. This was where Toy lived.

We approached Toy's place, a brick building one block long but with each segment painted a different color to pretend they were different houses. On the sidewalk, *covering* the sidewalk so you had to walk into the gutter to get around it, was a motorcycle. A whole lot of motorcycle. It was a Harley-Davidson police model, fully dressed, midnight blue with tiny silver star sparkles in it and the word *respect* written in ultra fine white script along the teardrop gas tank. Attached to it was a double piggyback sidecar. Automatically the three of us stopped and stared at the bike like we'd never seen anything like it before because, at least for Sully and me, we never had. Not so for Toy, though.

"That's my old man's," he said, the smile spreading wide despite his effort to cool it. "Sometimes I get to take it out myself."

If he wasn't lying, and I got the impression that Toy was one of those rare guys who never had to make stuff up, then he was now bigger than ever. Immense. I noticed Sully doing exactly what I was doing, running his eyes back from Toy to the bike, from the bike to Toy, getting it all together. It would take a major man to ride that machine, not just because it was huge and heavy, but because it had *bigness,* wildness all its own that no mortal high school kid could dream of tackling. If Toy could handle that . . .

I believed him.

"Come on up," he said as he pushed open the narrow door into the dark hallway. We walked up to the second floor where the landing forked into two apartment entrances before the stairway continued on up to the third and fourth floors. "You'll like my father," Toy said as he turned the old skeleton key, wiggling it around in the loose lock. "He's a little rough, but he's an all right guy."

Toy pushed open the door to give us all a full-on view of the sofa, where his big, black-bearded father sat facing the door shirtless, his legs spread out over the coffee table, one boot kicked off, his large pewter skull belt buckle dangling off a sofa cushion. He was squeezing two similarly barebacked women to his hairy chest. There was a lot of sweat on Toy's dad, a heavy man. There was a lot of sweat in the air, too. When we came in the women pulled closer in to him, covering up, refusing to turn even their faces. "Make them go," one whispered.

Toy's voice came out slow, low, measured. "I

should have called. I thought maybe we'd do some barbecue."

We had already started back down the stairs when Toy's father's voice followed us, deep and loud without his even yelling. Most definitely, the voice of the owner of that motorcycle. "We could do that, Toy. Come on, come on back up."

"Nah, don't worry about it," Toy said without breaking stride. "It was my fault, I should have called." He sounded a little disappointed, a little guilty, but that was it.

Back we went, through the neighborhoods, nobody talking, Sully and me staring at Toy's back, then dumbly at each other.

"You come to my house," I heard myself say. It was one of those situations where you just have to say something or you're all going to explode with the tension, so under pressure you say the stupidest thing you can think of. I could read from the glee on Sully's face that that's what I'd done.

"Ya? Me too?" Sully asked.

Having already defeated myself, all I could do was nod as I flashed forward to feeding my first new friend since probably first grade to my family.

Not that my mother wasn't as surprised as Toy's dad to see me strolling in with not one but two dinner guests, but she was also a little thrilled about it.

"Certainly, certainly," Ma said, "we can always stretch. Sit, boys, sit."

I winced as I asked, picturing my mother "stretching" a Swanson's Hungry Man Dinner, peeling back the foil, slicing down the salisbury steak, scooping out half of the little dollop of mashed potatoes to make two demi-dollops.

"Fish cakes," she chirped. "I'll pop open another can of beans and we'll be all set."

I breathed a little lighter. She always made about thirty fish cakes because my father went nuts for them. So tonight he'd have to settle for a dozen or so, which I didn't feel too guilty about.

"Isn't this nice," Ma said as she took her place at the table. She sat on one side, next to Sully, while Toy and I sat across from them. At one end of the table was an empty chair with food piled high in front of it—fish cakes stacked like tires, molasses-drenched baked beans oozing all over, and McCain's alphabet french fries. Because my father comes in promptly at six o'clock every night, give or take five minutes, and he likes to hit the ground running, supperwise. At the opposite end of the table was an empty seat with no plate. Because Terry comes home at the same time too, give or take a week.

Dad tromped through the kitchen, yanked open the refrigerator, pulled out a sixpack of Pabst Blue Ribbon, and plopped into his seat. He had an entire fish cake in his mouth before he noticed there were new people around him. He stopped chewing.

"Sully?" he said, half-greeting, half-question.

"Hi," Sully said, waving his fork.

Dad then turned to Toy. Stared at him as he returned to chewing. Silently, he pulled a beer off the ring and offered it to Toy, who shook his head no. He passed one to me, one to Sully, one to Ma, and cracked one for himself, leaving two beside his plate.

"He gets to have one on special occasions, when we have company," Ma said to Toy, remembering how old I was, remembering we had witnesses.

I leaned and whispered to Toy. "I get to have one when we have company. I get to have four when we don't."

"Sir, you wear a hat at the dinner table?" Dad asked.

Toy looked up, surprised. "No, sir, I don't," he said, and reached up for it.

Sully and I were riveted. We stared as he removed the hat.

There he was. He let the hat drop to the floor

beside him and looked around the table, a sort of, go-ahead-take-it-all-in look on his face. So I did. He had a large, strong Roman nose, olivy skin that looked somehow whiter than mine against his dark shadow beard, all of which you could see even with the hat but looked so much different now. His hair was standing up, something between a light brown and a gray, and so kinky nothing like a comb could bother it. But the stunners, the magnets, were his eyes, black. Black like marbles, black. And huge. Wide and soft, like a deer's eyes.

It was the eyes. Toy didn't like them, I realized. He tried to squint them, to harden them, but it was no use.

My father, I noticed, was looking at Toy so hard that I knew something was going to come out. I wasn't looking forward to it. He was gesturing, pointing with his finger and nodding like when you're trying to guess the answer to something that you know but it just won't come. He's a very simple man, my father, and I was terrified about what he might say.

"You a Greek?" Dad said.

"No," Toy said.

My mother interrupted. "Would you like something else to drink, Toy?"

"No, thank you."

"You a Jew? You ain't a Jew, are ya?"

"Dad," I popped. "Cut it out."

"What? I'm just askin'."

"That's right, Hank," Ma said. "Toy is all right whatever he is, even if he is Jewish. You're not, are you?"

"Jesus, *parents*," I said. "It's no wonder I never bring anybody here. Well, he ain't tellin' you what he is, so how do you like that?"

"I'll tell you what I am," Toy said evenly. Everyone else shut right up to hear it. Yes, I was as curious as the rest of them.

"I'm hungry, is what I am," he said. He stopped looking anybody in the face, concentrated on his plate. He ate some, played with his food some. He spelled ASS with his fries. My father drank down a beer in two swallows, drank another. Passed my mother another. Saw he was down to none, pulled another ring from the fridge and stuck it under his chair. Sully asked for and received another beer. I ate, tried to angle my head occasionally to get Toy to look at me, but no use.

Now what more could a party like this use?

Terry stumbled through the front door with a crash. We all listened to him ricochet off the walls as he made his way down the hall.

He didn't have to ask. A beer made its way

down the table to where Terry stared blankly at Sully, then at Toy.

"Do I know you?" Terry asked.

Toy barely turned his face up to respond. "No."

"I know you," Terry repeated.

"No, you don't know me," Toy answered with a deep chill on his voice.

Terry tipped his head back, pouring the beer in, some of it overflowing and running out of the corners of his mouth.

"I jus' thought I knew you, tha's all," Terry slurred before getting up again. "Thangs, Ma, dinner was pissa." He bounced back down the hall, slammed the door behind him.

"At least he doesn't bring none of his alky friends home with him," I said.

"Oh, I don't mind having alcoholics over for dinner," Ma said, sincere and generous as ever. "They can be sweet sometimes, some of them. The only thing is that they never know when to leave."

"Hey, I can take a hint," Sully said, and stood up. Ma laughed and pulled him back into his seat. "You're a cutup," she said.

Dad finished his fourth beer and his tenth fish cake. Those two things turned him into a much more jovial guy than the one who first sat down. "Babe, you're a delicious cook," he said to my mother. He reached out, took her hand, and licked her arm. "Delicious cook," he repeated, and laughed. Ma giggled like a kid.

Toy burrowed into his plate like they were not even there. Dad yanked one more beer for himself. "Can I have that?" I asked, pointing to the last one dangling off the ring. I wanted to bash myself in the temple with it as much as I wanted to drink it. But I drank it, of course.

"Come on, doll, we're gonna be late," Dad said, and he and Ma got up from the table. "Nice ta meet ya, kid," he said, shaking Toy's reluctant hand.

"We work at night, at a place called the O'Asis," Ma said. "Do you know it? Well anyway, we're going to own it soon."

"Thank you for dinner, ma'am," Toy said, standing as she stood.

As soon as my parents had left the house, Toy reached down and grabbed his hat. He jammed it way down on his head, making his ears fold over.

I didn't know what to say. I would have felt a whole lot better if we found my dad with half-naked women draped all over him.

Sully sauntered to the refrigerator for another beer, emboldened by the first two. I motioned for him to get me another one, is how I decided to approach this.

"So, Toy," Sul said. "Not that it really matters, but just to know, what are you, anyway?"

I got a quiver. Sully had no natural feeling for this kind of thing, for dealing with people. Toy pushed back his chair, stood, put his palms flat on the table, leaned way across in Sully's direction. "I'm a live human being," he said in a scary low rasp. "And if you ask me that question one more time you're going to be able to say you used to be one."

"I . . . I'll just take this to go," Sully said, raising the beer to us like a toast. "I'll see you guys tomorrow." And he ran.

I was humiliated. I was ashamed of my friend. I was ashamed of my brother. I was ashamed of my parents, of my food, of the stupid "God Bless Our Humble Home" plaque hanging, grease-encrusted, over the washing machine. I gulped my beer.

"Thank you for inviting me to your home," Toy said.

"They didn't mean anything," I said. "None of them. They just don't know nothing."

He waved it off. "So, how'd you like *my* house?"

I laughed because he made me feel better.

That and the beer, loosened me. "Your ma isn't around, I guess, huh?"

Toy patted me on the shoulder. It was the first time he had ever touched me, a fact that I realized at the instant of contact.

"The quiet one on the left was my ma," he said.

The Line in the Sand

"I heard somethin'," Terry said, shaking me awake.

"So, you heard something," I said, slapping his hand away.

He stood there over my bed, shaven, smelling of sweat and of everything he'd eaten and drunk the day before—knockwurst, onion rings, eggs, twelve different kinds of cheese, and, surprise, beer—ready for work in his baggy overalls and dark blue T-shirt with the pocket. Like a lot of other animals, Terry's a creature of habit. Shaving every single morning, but not showering until nighttime, sometimes not till three A.M., even if he smelled like goats. And he never left the house without a pocket T-shirt. He has ten of them, different colors.

"Augie tells me he seen you wit a undesirable," he said.

I tried to roll back over. "Go to work, will ya, Terry."

He grabbed my shoulder and ripped me back. "Name of Toy. You know who I'm talkin' about?"

"What do you care who I hang out with? Get yourself a life, for chrissake."

He paused, the pause that's supposed to mean he's being patient with me, letting me get away with something wise but that I better not do it again. "Thing is, that you're sorta my responsibility, lame or not, so I gotta look out for stuff, tell ya things. You're lucky ta have me, y'know."

"I *feel* lucky," I cracked. "I really do. I *want* you to tell me things, Terry. Tell me things like 'Goodbye,' or 'Adios,' or 'Ciao,' that would be nice." I didn't really care anymore what he thought, what he might do to me. I just wanted him the hell out of my room.

He went all cool, half for dramatic effect, half because he had no idea how to handle backtalk. "Okay then, since neither one of us seems to have the time for this bullshit, let me just tell ya, Mick. Be careful who you spend your time with.

It's one a the important rules of hangin' out: associatin' with bad news is pretty much the same as bein' bad news y'self. So even a innocent little shit like you can sometimes get a little a what we might call a spillover burn from bein' a little too close to somebody who's a little too hot. Knowatamean, boy?"

He smiled, that rotten little goddamn yellow-tooth smile as he waited for me to react. I wanted to throw it in his face that he sat right across the table from Toy in his own house and he didn't even figure it out. I wanted to ask him what his problem was with Toy anyhow, almost asked even, except I knew what a stupid question that would be. Did he need a reason? Did he ever need reason to start this kind of bullshit with somebody? No, the only thing that really stuck with me here, the only thing that seemed really different from anything before, was that my brother this time was *threatening* me. Not "I'm gonna break your head if you don't shut up," which he'd said and meant a million times before, not "Gimme five bucks, I'll pay ya back when I'm good and ready," not " . . . and don't tell nobody what ya just seen or you're a dead man," which ended many of our conversations. No, this one was different. This one was the real one, because he was questioning whether I was

on the team anymore—or if I was now the oppo-
sition. This one was the line in the sand, where if
I crossed, there was no connection anymore, no
responsibility, no rules, no limits. He was sort of
giving me the opportunity to resign from being
his brother, with all the *stuff* that would imply.
Serious stuff.

"Thank you," I said evenly. "For the advice, I
mean."

Terry left quietly, looking pleased, which
meant he thought our conversation went a different way than I thought it went. He thought it
went the way it always went before. His will be
done.

"Kiss me, Terry," I said, making a loud smack-
ing sound with my lips. "*I'll* give you undesirable. I got your 'whatcha might call spillover
burn,' right here, ya goddamn ape."

It felt good to say it. Kind of lifted me right
up off the bed to hear myself. It would have been
even better if Terry were still there to hear it.
Next time, I promised myself. Next time he will
be. He was there for the important part, though.
The thank-you. I meant it when I said thank you
to him. Because what he was telling me, it was
almost as if somebody was telling me I was, or
could be, who I wanted to be. Which, basically,
was not Terry. God, I wanted to be *not* Terry.

Kind of a hoot, after all, that the one to tell me was Terry himself.

Toy didn't think the story was nearly as funny as I did.

"I don't like anybody talking about me, good or bad, even mentioning my name, when I'm not there. Never liked it. Never liked it. Don't want to know about it."

"Ya but it's just my ignorant brother. He's not as big shit as he thinks he is. You don't take it seriously."

Toy shook his head, shook his hat. "Very seriously," he said.

"I think he's right," Sully said. "I think they mean business."

I leaned way over forward on my milk crate, looking past Toy to see Sul. We'd taken to hanging out in front of the store most afternoons now, me and Sul flanking Toy, crouched on milk crates, backs to the wall under the CHEAPEST MILK AND CIGARETTES IN TOWN sign. We smoked cigars like Toy did, chewed the occasional Slim Jim, talked for long stretches, played backgammon, and didn't talk for long stretches. Just to do it, to be *seen* doing it, protected in our raunchy brown tobacco cloud.

"What do you *know*, Sully?" I demanded.

Like I said, Sully is no natural at reading people. So if he pipes in that he thinks Terry means something by his words, it's because he's heard something.

"I heard something," Sully said.

"Cough it up," I said.

"Well, it was the last time Augie beat me up, last Tuesday or Wednesday. The stuff he was sayin' when he was slapping me—he's always sayin' something when he's slapping me, y'know, so it takes forever; I hate that."

"Sul?" I said, getting more anxious. I figured Toy was too, but he wasn't showing a thing. Not even interest.

"Oh, so he's cuffin' me, saying, 'And next time I catch your ass, if you're hangin' wit' that big Spaniel bastard, don't go thinkin' that'll save ya, 'cause that'll just mean you're gonna get what *he* gets. And he's got a muthuh *party* comin'. Take a note, little man.' And you know, I couldn't figure what big Spaniel bastard he coulda been talkin' about that I would be hangin' with, so I guess he must have just screwed up and meant Toy. 'Cause Toy is big, and he is a bastard."

Toy laughed at that, leaned his head back against the wall, making his hat go even further down over his face. I looked at him, looked for him to be nervous. But he wouldn't show it. I turned back to Sully, who would.

"Toy?" Sully asked cautiously. "Not for nothin', you understand, but what if . . . say you knew something like that was gonna happen, like this afternoon?"

"*This* afternoon?" I cut in.

"Like, just suppose. What do you suppose you might do, if you knew?"

Toy chewed on the cigar, rolling it around in his mouth a bit. "I guess I'd just do what I'm doing right now." He shrugged.

I couldn't be that casual. "So, Sul, what are you gonna do?" I asked, kind of asking myself by asking him.

Sully tilted his head sideways, looked off into space, like he hadn't thought about it before. Then he returned with his answer, turning back to me and shrugging, with a simpleton smile. "Well, I'm *here*, ain't I? That's doing something, I think."

Toy reached over and smacked Sully lightly on the side of the head, laughing again. He was right. For Sully—not the moxiest ol' boy around—staying to hang with Toy under the circumstances was something. Which seemed to leave only me with a crisis of nerve.

"Maybe we should do something else for a

change, y'know, not just hang out here on the same old sidewalk, in plain view, where everybody knows we're here. . . . How 'bout a movie? Or bowling, maybe."

"Take off if you want to, Mick," Toy said. "I understand. It won't bother me."

This was a problem for me. Toy just would not give it up, and now I was coming up even bigger chicken than Sully. Which was *big* chicken. "God, will you stop being so cool and collected all the time, Toy? I hate that. Doesn't this stuff have any effect on you at all? Don't you feel anything—"

"Got a quarter?" Toy cut in.

"Huh?"

"For a phone call. I have no change."

"Goddamn it, Toy," I said, hopping to my feet, waving my arms in front of him.

He got up, stood toe to toe with me. Calmly but firmly he said, "I won't discuss animals. I don't care what they do. I won't waste not one of my days thinking about them. I won't." He extended his palm for the coin.

"I got it," Sully said, flipping the money up to Toy, who walked the few paces to the pay phone on the wall by the store entrance.

"He's a friggin' cuke, ain't he," Sully asked as we both watched Toy.

"*He* is? Since when have you been such a cool cucumber, being so stand-up after Augie warned you?"

"Ya," Sully said, nodding in amazement as if we were talking about some third party who was not himself, "where did that shit come from? Must be Toy. Something contagious about him."

Toy was waving me over to the phone. I went, as did Sully, who was not invited but never needed to be.

"It's for you," Toy said, jamming the receiver into my hand. "Evelyn."

I froze, with the phone a foot away from my ear. Suddenly I was thirsty, as if an entire cylinder of Morton's salt had been poured down my gullet. I was vaguely aware of Sully's low laughter about a thousand miles behind me, and I heard myself making a scratchy throat-clearing sound.

"Get *on* with it," Toy said, reaching out and bending my arm for me to bring the phone to my ear.

"Hello?" I said, though it was still ringing.

"*Hola*," the voice came on. My throat closed even tighter when I realized it was Evelyn's brother, Ruben.

"Ah, can I speak to Evelyn?"

This was followed by a long silence.

"Who is this?" he finally said suspiciously.

I knew answering that question wouldn't help. So I didn't. "Could I please—"

Click.

I asked Toy for the number and Sully for the coin, and called right back before losing my new-found nerve.

"Buenos días," he said brightly, picking up on the first ring.

"Hello, I'd like to speak to—"

Click.

Sully and Toy were all subdued smiles when I slammed the receiver down.

"Shut up," I said.

"I think maybe I can make you a little head-way here," said Toy. He took up the phone.

"Hola," he said after a short wait. *"¿Es posible hablar a Evelyn, por favor? Sí. No, no se. ¿Mick? Hmmm, no, Mick no está conmigo. ¿Ella es allí? Maravilloso."*

I looked at Sully. Sully looked at me.

"Gracias," Toy said, then turned to me. "You're on."

I took the phone again, fuzzy again. I was thinking as much about Toy now as I was about Evelyn. Spanish? Why didn't I know that? Had I said anything ignorant that might have offended him, back before I knew? Sully, Toy's good buddy just minutes before, was standing three feet away from him now, looking most confused. Evelyn took her sweet time coming to the phone. I thought I heard something.

"Olé," I said, but she wasn't there yet.

"The word is *hola*," Toy said, disgusted. "Don't even try. I think English is enough of a chore for you."

"Yes?" Her soft but very serious voice came over the line.

"Ya, hello, Evelyn. Hi."

"Who is this, please?" she said, a lot more suspiciously than she needed to. I was slipping away already, I could feel it.

"How 'bout could we talk first, and *then* I could tell you who I am?"

"If you don't tell me who you are right now, I'm hanging up."

"It's Mick."

Click.

"Well, you got a couple of sentences deeper than I thought you'd get," Toy said. "It's a promising start."

"And finish," I said. "It's unbelievable, how much I'm hated by that girl. I can actually *feel* it, the hate, when I'm near her. It's not a good feeling, Toy."

"You're doing fine," Toy said, sticking a cigar in my direction. "She just doesn't know you yet. She will like what's inside, when she sees it. Trust me."

I took the cigar, pointed it back at him like a teacher's pointer. "You know her. I mean, *really* know her, don't you?"

He lit up his cigar with a sly grin, gripping it in his teeth. "I know lots of things," he said.

Toy offered a cigar to Sully, who had been staring dumbly at him since the phone thing. He didn't take it. "You speak Spanish," Sully said flatly.

"I speak Spanish," Toy repeated, same tone.

"How come you never spoke it around us before?"

"*¿Porqué no hablas Español alrededor de mí?*"

"What does it matter, Sul? This is Toy, for chrissake. What are you thinking?"

"I don't know, Mick. Toy, I don't know what I'm thinkin'. But I'm thinkin' *something*. I mean, a guy just wants to know these things about another guy, that's all. I don't know. A guy shouldn't hide stuff, that's all. Y'know, for trust, he shouldn't."

"*I don't hide,*" Toy said, mean enough to scare me.

"*I don't agree,*" Sully answered, not nearly as tough, but pretty aggressive for Sully.

We all stood looking each other over for a minute. It was weird, like we were meeting for the first time all over again. It started out as another Toy-Sully thing, but I was doing it too. It was uncomfortable.

"I'm gonna go," Sully said. "I'll catch you all."

We didn't say anything to him, not even good-bye, because nothing would have been quite right then. It was good for him to go, and it was good for us to move on to something else.

"You think you have the guts to see this thing through?" Toy asked, trying to sound light.

"Which thing?"

"Miss Evelyn?"

I got the butterflies again. I nodded.

"Let's go pay her a visit."

"At her *house*?" I said. "No, Toy, I know you know her and you know everything about everything and all, but, no, I can't go *there*."

"Why not?"

"Why not? 'Cause I got a problem, is why not. A reputation, a stigma, a bullseye on my ass, is why not. And if I do make it through the neighborhood all the way to Evelyn's house, she'll shoot me herself right there on her doorstep."

Toy laughed at me and started pulling me along by the arm. "*I* can take you there," he said.

"You'll be fine. What the lady needs from you is sincerity, she likes sincerity. You go there, show her the effort, she'll see you're sincere. The door will open. Trust me."

I badly wanted that door to open. And I did trust Toy. Even if he did hide things.

Spillover Burn

The dumb monkey, I waddled along behind Toy as he led me just like that to the place I so wanted to go. He walked the way he always walked, medium slow, side-to-side rock, but looking straight on, with purpose. I followed roughly in his steps, but looking everywhere else. My nerves were acting up again. It was a case of wanting to *be* at Evelyn's house without having to *get* there.

Old men sat on stools outside the six-table restaurant, the *Boca Loca*. The overwhelming smell of garlic and cinnamon rolling out the open door somehow came together and made sense, made me hungry, made me calmer. We passed Soraya's Children's Boutique with silly-looking tiny versions of adult clothes on scary gnomish mannequins in the front window and nobody inside. We passed the bowling alley that sounded like thunder with the twenty-candlepin lanes and *Los Violines* nightclub—"Open All Day" —right next door, playing salsa out of a gigantic jukebox and advertising THE AMAZING RUBEN BLADES AND SON DEL SOLAR, on a life-sized concert poster. Under the poster was tacked a hand-lettered sign, "He ain't gonna be here, but we like him anyway."

When we hit Pablo's Complex of Beauty, it was time to turn off Centre Street onto South. Evelyn's street. On one corner three men were taking parts off a new white five-liter Mustang and transferring them to an old, red one. On the other corner was a phone company van.

I had never been down South Street. I didn't even *know* anyone who had walked down South Street. And I guess South Street sort of saw me the same way. I got some *looks*. I recognized guys from school, walking past, sitting on cars or on steps. People who just didn't bother with me at school, but now, here, shot me the intense, no-fooling look. Most just nodded, or grunted, respectful-like, at Toy as he cleared me a path.

"Almost to the promised land," Toy said over

his shoulder. "Place with the pink door there, with the Mary-on-the-half-shell in the yard."

We were almost there, approaching the statues—Mary standing in an upturned bathtub, draped in flowers and surrounded by pink flamingos standing on one leg. There were a lot of other Mary statues around, but this was the slickest. It made me smile, which helped the raging butterflies that were overtaking me. Suddenly, something else overtook me, from the street side.

The phone truck that had been parked at the end of the street two blocks back was here now. And not parked, but moving beside us. Creeping. At exactly our pace. I stopped, peered right into it.

"Shiiit!" I yelled. "Toy, we gotta run." I pulled his sleeve, but he yanked it out of my hand.

"What for? I ain't running nowhere." He puffed up a bit, made two fists and looked in all directions.

Doors popped open all over the van. The front passenger side, sliding side door, back doors. Out came Augie, Danny, one fat Cormac— the other stayed at the wheel—and a more-than-typically-demented-looking Baba.

"All right, cut the shit now," I said, holding up my hands and walking toward them.

"Where's my brother?" What did I think, that I could *fix* everything? By *talking?* To *Terry?* There was no Terry anyway. He would be home, at the Bloody, pulling the strings and obeying his restraining order.

They didn't even acknowledge me. Augie in the lead, pulled a cop nightstick from behind his back, dipped a shoulder into me and bounced me aside. Then Baba came along, his eyes red-rimmed tiny black dots. He wore something on his fist, like a dog chain with the links welded together to fit perfectly, rigidly across the knuckles. "Come on, Baba," I pleaded, trying to tap into something that wasn't there.

He walked right over me. Literally, like in war clips on the news when the tanks roll right over the tiny people. So wired he showed no comprehension of who I was or that I was rolling under his feet. So died a lifetime friendship.

I looked up to see Augie walk to Toy—who of course had not taken a single backward step—and raise the nightstick. Before Augie even had the thing over his head, Toy shot him a rocket right hand, out of nowhere, no windup, no crouch, no leverage, that picked up boosters out of the air and *dropped* Augie like a sack of soup bones to the sidewalk. The nightstick clacked across the cement. Toy stood. His feet never even shifted. I got back to my feet, but stood there like a spectator.

"Too long, too long," Cormac called, sticking his head out the van window. "Gotta go." No one was particularly concerned with Augie holding his face and rolling on the sidewalk.

Baba stepped up to Toy, raised his chain-encrusted fist, turning it around and back again, admiring it.

Finally, Toy took a step back. He reached around behind him, down into his pants.

Shik. The blade, six inches, was out and up, between them. Baba moved on him anyway.

"Take off, Toy," I said. He stood there.

"Let's *go!*" Cormac yelled, putting the van in gear.

Then there was a click. The tiny noise that shot through everything else. We all looked to see Danny with the gun pointed Toy's way. His hand was shaking, and I would have bet anything he couldn't do it. But there it was.

"Go," I yelled at Toy. "They ain't gonna bother me. *Go!*"

Toy hesitated, then ran, his boots clicking loudly down the street. I thought Danny was going to faint, he looked so drained and relieved as he let the gun swing down at his side. He helped Augie to his feet and they all started piling into the van. "We ain't lettin' him get away," Augie muttered.

"Let him go," Cormac the driver said. "We made him shit his pants, that's what's important." Like the rest of them, Cormac was not as hot about the operation as Augie was. Like *most* of the rest of them, anyway.

"Waste 'im. Waste 'im," Baba growled through gritted teeth. He was walking past me, the last to get back to the van. He stopped, stared down at me, and if he recognized me this time, he sure didn't show it. But he was fired with hate anyway.

Crash. And *crash* again. The first being Baba's big fist, big as my face, coming down on the side of my head, the chain links pressing their shape into the bone. The second was me hitting the sidewalk.

Run, Toy, they won't bother me. How many times could I be wrong? How little did I know about everything now?

I couldn't see it, but I heard the van tear away, down the street in the direction Toy ran. "Hope the natives make Spaniel chow outta ya," one of them called.

Then there was silence. I opened my eyes. They closed again. I opened them again. My cheek was pressed against the grainy pavement, most of my weight supported by the side of my head and my shoulder as I lay crumpled, my ass in the air. I blinked to focus, blinked to focus, got something a little clearer each time, but not good. Two sets of blurry feet walked right by me without even a hitch for the curiosity.

Then the door opened on the porch closest to me, the door I had come to open in the first place. As Evelyn took a few steps out, I made my eyes wider and wider to see her. She stood there looking down, her bare feet hanging over the top step. She was wearing a white gauzy Communion-type dress, almost to her ankles. Her feet bare. She was brushing her hair hand-over-hand, pulling it down over the front of her shoulder with one hand, brushing it out with the other, pulling it down, brushing it out. Casually, like she had all day to do it.

I struggled, pushed off the ground, wrestled myself up to sitting position. I steadied myself by putting one hand flat on the ground, while with the other I tried to smooth and straighten my hair.

There was a haze around Evelyn, one of my eyes being washed with the blood, the other with, I guess, tears. I would blink it away, but in seconds it would be back, and she would be floating again. When I thought my hair was nice, I tried to smile at her, instead toppled back over, my head pressing again to the sidewalk. I tried to get up but I couldn't do it.

"Well, at least we got one of them," she said, her dress whirling as she turned back toward the door.

"I'm not one of them," I said, closing my eyes.